TO HONOR

THE MCNALLYS

LAURA SCOTT

READSCAPE PUBLISHING, LLC

1

Jesse McNally headed into Daisy's Diner, enjoying the familiarity of the place. Daisy's hadn't changed over the past nine years since the last time he'd spent the summer at his grandparents' house with his siblings.

He'd been eighteen, nearly nineteen, and leaving for college in the fall and hadn't returned to McNally Bay for any real length of time other than the occasional visit over the holidays.

Until now.

Grandma and Grandpa McNally had passed away within four months of each other earlier in the year. His twin sisters, Jazz and Jemma, had turned their grandparents' mansion into a thriving new business, the McNallys' B&B. Jazz and Dalton had gotten married this past weekend, their ceremony taking place in the white gazebo overlooking Lake Michigan.

Jesse decided to extend his visit for a week, needing a break after the recent and incredibly complex software restoration he'd managed for Avery and Arch Accounting.

The company he'd cofounded with his college roommate, Brian Malone, was called Software Solutions, Inc. After six weeks of working seven days a week, ten hours a day, to combat the horrible bout of ransomware that had held Avery and Arch hostage, he deserved a break.

"Well, if it isn't Jesse McNally!" Betty Cromwell was the first to greet him when he walked in. She sat at a booth near the doorway, beaming up at him. She was always dressed the same, in a flowery dress and low heels, even in the heat of summer. Her hair was a riot of gray curls that hung in disarray around her face. "It's good you decided to stick around for a while."

He grinned and bent down to give the town gossip a quick peck on the cheek. "You haven't changed a bit since the last time I saw you," he declared.

Betty giggled like a schoolgirl and waved her hand at him. "That doesn't mean much since I just saw you Saturday at Jazz and Dalton's wedding." She lowered her voice to a conspiratorial tone. "The only reason they're together is because of me."

"Really? How so?" It didn't surprise him that Betty Cromwell was taking credit for the wedding, but he hadn't heard the story of how Dalton and Jazz had met. The B&B had been chaotic since all six siblings had been together for the first time in over two years. Jeremy had come over from Lansing, and even Jake had flown in from Ireland.

"Dalton did some handyman work for me, repairing my bathroom, and I happened to mention how Jazz was renovating her grandparents' home on the lake. I encouraged him to visit Jazz to see if she was willing to hire him to help with the construction project. He was a drifter at the time, you see, so I gave him a good reference. Jazz hired him." Betty nodded sagely, her gray curls dancing around her plump face, and spread her hands wide. "The rest is history!"

He chuckled. "I guess it is. I like Dalton. He does great work. Did you see the garage apartment they built for Jemma and Trey? It's amazing. And it's clear Dalton and Jazz are very much in love."

"Well now, there's still time for the rest of you McNally boys to find someone." Betty patted his arm. "Look at your brother Jonas. He found Bella at the McNallys' Bed and Breakfast, and now they're incredibly happy together."

Jesse nodded and tried not to roll his eyes. He liked Mrs. Cromwell but wasn't interested in being the subject of her not-so-subtle matchmaking. His girlfriend recently left him for someone else. Turned out to be a guy named Wade Nolan who didn't work long hours during software security breaches or travel from one city and state to the next, providing computer expertise. Jesse wasn't exactly heart-broken over Paula's breakup, but he wasn't looking to get involved again either.

"No need to worry about me. I'm fine on my own, Ms. Cromwell," he assured her.

As he spoke, a woman sitting three booths behind Betty caught his eye. He stared in surprise, recognizing his teenage crush, Carla Templeton. What was she doing here, in McNally Bay? She looked amazing, and he felt his pulse kick up a notch. "Excuse me." He left Mrs. Cromwell to move toward his teenage flame.

"Carla." He was shocked at the nervous squeak in his voice and did his best to sound normal. "How are you?"

Carla looked up at him with a tight smile that didn't reach her eyes. "Jesse. I heard you were in town for your sister's wedding."

"Yeah, uh, wow. It's great to see you." His heart thudded

painfully against his ribs as he absorbed the fact that the young girl he'd once loved had grown into a stunningly beautiful woman. Her long auburn hair was pulled away from her heart-shaped face, and her green eyes were as bright as he remembered. Carla was still slender, yet she seemed to have gained more curves than when they were younger. It made him smile to remember how they used to sneak out after curfew to meet down at the lakefront to kiss, talk, and discuss their hopes and dreams for the future. "It would be great to catch up. Mind if I join you?"

"Oh, I'm sorry, but you can't." She put her hand out as if to ward him off. "I'm meeting someone for lunch." Carla's expression turned wary as she glanced nervously over her shoulder. He thought it strange as the front door to the diner was behind him, not her. "Listen, I only have a short break for lunch, then I need to get back to work. Please excuse me." She looked past him, lifting a hand to flag down the busy waitress.

"What can I get you, Carla?" A blond woman, wearing a nametag that read Ashley, plunked two glasses of water on the table, then pulled a notepad out of her apron pocket.

"We'll have the usual, thanks, Ashley." Carla looked at him one last time. "Enjoy your visit with your family."

The dismissive tone in Carla's voice put him on edge. A glance at the ring finger of her left hand confirmed she wasn't wearing an engagement or wedding ring, but that didn't necessarily mean anything. He wasn't sure where Carla worked, but it could be somewhere that didn't allow jewelry.

Was she living in McNally Bay now? When they were young, she'd wanted nothing more than to get away.

He gave himself a mental shake. What did he care? It wasn't as if he was planning to move back to McNally Bay anytime soon. Their intense but brief bout of puppy love had burned out when they'd both gone their separate ways. He'd gone to the University of Wisconsin–Madison while she'd been accepted at the University of Iowa. They'd promised to keep in touch and had for a few weeks, until the distance and adjustment to being in college had gotten in the way.

Carla turned and rummaged in her purse, no doubt as a way to convince him to move along. It wasn't difficult to figure out she was meeting a man for lunch and didn't want or need him hanging around.

"Good to see you, Carla." He waited for her to acknowledge him before turning away.

"Take care, Jesse." She didn't meet his gaze and again glanced nervously over her shoulder. Maybe the guy joining her was in the restroom.

Disappointed, he moved away and looked for someplace to sit. Glancing at the counter, he noticed there was one open spot. He made his way toward the stool when a young girl who looked to be around eight or nine years old, with the same auburn hair as Carla's, came running toward the booth from somewhere in the back of the diner.

"Mom! Guess what? Miss Daisy said I could earn some money walking her dog each day! Now in the summer, and once I'm back in school."

Mom? Jesse frowned and watched as the girl slid into the seat across from Carla.

"She'll pay me five dollars to walk Bucky for an hour every day," the girl continued. "It's going to be awesome. I'm going to save up enough money to buy my own phone."

"That's great, Cassie." From where Jesse stood, he could tell Carla was shifting uncomfortably in her seat while studiously avoiding his gaze.

A sick feeling washed over him as he studied the girl. Her features were exactly like those of her mother, auburn hair, porcelain skin, and green eyes, but her gestures and mannerisms reminded him of Jazz.

He stared in shock. No. It couldn't be. Could it?

"Carla?" He hadn't realized he'd called her name out loud until she turned to look at him.

The guilt shadowing her green gaze was all it took. In that instant, he knew.

Cassie was his daughter.

NOOOO!

Carla's silent scream echoed in her mind as realization dawned in Jesse's dark gaze. In a heartbeat, he came toward them with a glint of fire in his eyes, and she did her best to ward him off with a narrow glare.

"I'm sorry, Jesse, but this isn't a good time." She managed to keep her voice level yet stern. "Maybe we can talk later?"

"When?" Jesse demanded as he loomed over her. She wanted to jump to her feet and push him back, but she knew that would only cause a scene.

As if they weren't making a spectacle of themselves already. Carla felt several pairs of curious eyes, including Betty Cromwell's, staring at them. News of this meeting was going to spread around town faster than flies swarmed fresh meat.

She'd never told anyone who Cassie's father was. Especially not her parents. Her father had been so upset upon finding out she was pregnant he'd slapped her across the face, screaming at her that the father better not be one of those no-good McNallys. Less than five minutes later, he'd clutched his chest, going sweaty and pale. He'd crumpled to the floor while she'd called 911 and then began performing CPR. Her father had made it to the nearest hospital but had never woken up. He'd died a week later, leaving a heavy sense of guilt that lingered to this day.

"Mom? Is something wrong?" Cassie asked, picking up on the tension between the adults.

"Not at all." She tried to paste a smile on her face. She needed Jesse to pipe down or the entire town would know the truth before sundown. She glanced up at Jesse. "I get off work at eight o'clock tonight. We can talk then, okay?"

Jesse didn't look happy with the delay but too bad. There was nothing she could do to change it. She'd taken over managing the grocery store two years ago, after her mom had been diagnosed with breast cancer. Meals with Cassie were the only indulgence she allowed herself these days.

And she wasn't about to let Jesse ruin this one.

"Fine," he finally agreed. "Where can I pick you up?"

She didn't want to admit she lived in the same house she'd grown up in. "I'll meet you at Gino's."

Jesse hesitated, then nodded curtly. His gaze lingered for a moment on Cassie, and she knew he wanted to be introduced. "Cass, this is an old friend of mine, Jesse McNally. Jesse, my daughter, Cassandra."

"Hi." Cassie smiled up at him. "Do you live in the McNally Mansion?"

Cassie's blunt question caused Jesse's features to relax into a smile. "No, I live in Chicago, but my sister Jemma lives there. It's not a mansion anymore, though. It's a bed and breakfast."

"What's that?" Cassie asked, ever the curious one.

"Like a hotel, only the guests are offered free breakfast in the morning," Carla explained.

"Cool." Cass seemed to take the explanation in stride. "Nice to meet you, Mr. McNally."

"Please call me . . ." Jesse's voice trailed off, and he once again caught her gaze. She stiffened in her seat. There was no way in the world she was getting into this discussion now. No matter how much this older adult version of Jesse reminded her of happier times.

"You may call him Mr. Jesse," she said to her daughter.

"Okay. Bye, Mr. Jesse."

"Nice to meet you, Cassie." Jesse's eyes looked suspiciously moist as he turned away. Carla twisted her hands together under the table, trying to comprehend what had just happened.

She'd briefly considered leaving with Cassie for a few days while Jesse was in town, but July was the height of tourist season for McNally Bay, and the grocery store was exceptionally busy. Besides, she never expected Jesse would stick around long enough to run into her. Much less, see Cassie.

But he had. And now he knew the truth. Even worse, it was clear he had no intention of leaving them alone.

He looked the same, yet different. Older and wiser? Maybe. Yet the moment she'd caught a whiff of his after-shave, she'd shivered as memories washed over her.

No. She couldn't, wouldn't deal with this now. She took a sip of her water and eyed her daughter across the table. "Tell me, Cass, what kind of dog is Bucky?"

"He's a Goldendoodle, which means he's part Golden retriever and part poodle," her daughter explained. "But not a small poodle, a big one. He has golden curly hair and is super friendly. Miss Daisy says he's a puppy with lots of energy, so I'm supposed to take him for really long walks each day."

"I see." Carla wasn't really thinking about Bucky as she toyed with her Cobb salad. Her appetite had vanished, and despite how she loved sharing meals with her daughter, her mind was already preoccupied with the upcoming confrontation with Jesse. The secret she'd carried for nine long years was about to come out in the worst way.

And like a freight train barreling straight toward her, there was nothing she could do to stop it.

Cassie eagerly dipped her breaded chicken strips in ketchup. "She said I can play with him during the summer any time I want."

"Hmm." Carla wondered what Jesse wanted out of this meeting. After all this time, did he really think he could just snap his fingers and become a father to their daughter? She didn't want or need his money. The grocery store was doing fine, and she'd remained living with her mother out of convenience rather than for financial reasons. When Cassie had been a baby, her mother had helped her out, babysitting and giving her a job. After her mother's six-month fight with breast cancer and chemo, their roles had reversed and Carla was the one helping to take care of her mother.

"Mom? You're not listening."

"Huh?" She shot a guilty look at her daughter. "You're right, I'm sorry. I was distracted. What did you say?"

Cassie flashed an impish smile. "I said that Miss Daisy said I can bring Bucky home to live with us forever."

"Cass, you know that Miss Daisy only asked you to help with Bucky, not adopt him." She forced herself to take a bite of her salad.

"I know." Cassie was a good-natured kid. "Too bad Grandma's allergic to dogs or we could get one of our own."

"Just think, you'll get to have fun times with Bucky without the constant work of caring for him." The request for a dog wasn't anything new, and she was glad her daughter would be able to spend quality time with Bucky while earning a little money, too. Not for a phone, eight-year-old children were too young to have their own phones, but for something else.

"If Mr. Jesse is your friend, how come I haven't seen him before?" Cass asked.

She hesitated, caught off guard by the question. "I knew him a long time ago, before you were born. We haven't kept in touch over the years."

"Does he want to ask you out for a date, the way Mr. Thomas does?"

"What? No! Of course not. Where did you hear that?" She set down her fork, wondering how in the world Cass heard that her school principal, Dean Thomas, had asked her out on a date? They'd only had a cup of coffee, nothing more, and while Dean had made it clear he was interested, she couldn't find the enthusiasm or the time to continue seeing him.

"Grandma told me." Cass popped a French fry in her mouth.

"Grandma has a big mouth." Her mother had made it clear that she wanted to see Carla happily married before she died. Not that her mother was going to die anytime soon. At her last checkup, the oncologist had deemed her cancer free. Still, it was annoying to know her mother had talked with her daughter about her love life.

Or lack thereof.

"We're just friends," Carla repeated firmly. "And you need to stop listening to Grandma. She's the one who wants a son-in-law. I'm too busy for that stuff."

Cass frowned. "But, Mom, I don't want you to be alone

either. And Grandma said you always push men off because you'd rather be alone."

It was disconcerting to hear her daughter talking about relationships. "Honey, trust me. When I find a man I can't live without, I'll marry him. Okay? Now let's change the subject."

Before either one of them could say anything more, there was a loud crash from outside.

Diner patrons glanced at each other in confusion, before looking through the windows to see what was going on in the small parking lot in front of the diner.

"Jesse. Isn't that your car?" Mrs. Cromwell asked in a loud voice.

Jesse jumped off his stool and headed out the door. Carla craned her neck to watch as he approached a sporty red car. It looked like a Corvette, and she remembered how he'd always wanted a little red Corvette, just like the song.

She gasped when she noticed the windshield had been shattered into millions of tiny pieces. Jesse opened the passenger side door and pulled out a large brick. He hefted it in his hand and glanced around the area as if trying to figure out who'd thrown it at his car.

She covered her mouth in horror. Someone had trashed Jesse McNally's car on purpose.

Who would do such a thing? And why?

2

Jesse did his best to rein in his anger as he waited for the sheriff's deputy to arrive. Kids could be jerks, and he had to believe that a couple of kids who were jealous of his nice sports car had decided to trash it with a brick.

It wasn't that he couldn't afford to pay for the repairs, but it was more about the inconvenience. The Corvette was a classic. He'd have to take the car to Chicago to get the windshield replaced.

He heard a low whistle and turned to see his future brother-in-law, Sheriff's Deputy Garth Lewis, staring at his damaged car with a pained expression on his face.

"That's not right," Garth said, shaking his head sadly. "A classic like that deserves better."

"Yeah, tell me about it." Jesse tried not to show the depths of his anger. "Thanks for coming. I need a police report for my insurance company."

Garth nodded. "I know. Anyone see what happened?"

Jesse had asked around, but no one had come forward with information. "Not that they've told me."

"You piss someone off?" Garth persisted.

He glanced back at Daisy's Diner, knowing the only person who'd recently expressed anger toward him was Carla. She and Cassie had their faces pressed to the window, watching with blatant curiosity. But as they'd been inside at the time of the brick sailing through his windshield, he shook his head. "Not that I know of."

"Hmm." Garth's expression turned guarded, and Jesse followed the deputy's gaze to where a man, leaning heavily on a cane, stood off to the side next to a woman who may have been his daughter. There was no mistaking the satisfied smirk on his face.

Did the old guy have something against Corvettes?

Before Jesse could ask about the old man, Garth approached him. They had a low conversation during which the old guy scowled and shook his head before walking away with his younger companion.

"What was that about?"

Garth sighed. "Leon Tate and his daughter, Mary, have been harboring a grudge against the McNally family for a long time. Goes back to when your father was young."

"So he threw a brick at my car?" Jesse curled his fingers into fists. "Then he can pay for the damage."

Garth held up a hand. "Hold on, I don't have any proof that Leon or Mary Tate did this. Leon claims he and his daughter had just arrived at the diner when they noticed you standing out here in front of your damaged car. And before you ask, no, they didn't see anyone who may have done this."

"Yeah, like I believe that," Jesse muttered. "Based on what I saw, they wouldn't tell us even if they had seen someone suspicious. Why does Tate hate our father anyway? Mom and Dad have been gone for several years. Seems like a long time to hold a grudge."

"Longer than you know," Garth responded on a heavy sigh. "You should talk to Jazz and Jemma about it. They're the ones putting the story together piece by piece. Right now, I need to do my job."

"Yeah, fine." Jesse grimaced at the damage to his car. He didn't think it would be a good idea to drive the car all the way to Chicago without a windshield, so he pulled out his phone to arrange for a tow truck. The cost of having the Corvette towed to Chicago would probably be more than replacing the stupid windshield.

"I'll give you a lift home," Garth offered once he'd finished making the arrangements.

"Thanks." While he waited for Garth, he went inside to leave cash for his tab at the diner. Since he knew Carla wouldn't talk to him until their meeting later tonight, he thought he may as well head back to the B&B. He glanced back at the window, hoping to catch another glimpse of them, but Carla and Cassie Templeton were gone.

He was still reeling from the news that Carla had gotten pregnant all those years ago. They'd been careful and had only slipped up a couple of times. But still, why hadn't she told him? She had to have known he wouldn't have shirked his responsibilities.

He felt like an idiot that he hadn't known about his daughter. Hadn't helped raise her or pay for anything. Carla had stolen that time he could have spent with his daughter by not reaching out to him. She knew he was attending University of Wisconsin–Madison. Why hadn't she called?

Of course, he hadn't called her either. Especially after talking about the possibility of getting together over homecoming weekend. As the weeks had passed, he'd gotten caught up with his new friends and hadn't called Carla back.

At the same time, he was secretly glad his parents weren't around to hear the news. Even at this age, if his dad was still here, he'd have boxed his ears. And Jesse wouldn't blame him.

Cassandra was adorable, and he wanted to get to know his daughter better. The way Carla had acted so strangely in the diner convinced him that his daughter had no idea she was related to anyone who'd once spent summer vacations at the McNally Mansion.

"Hey, don't take it too hard," Garth said, misinterpreting his silence. "I hate to say it but look on the bright side. A damaged windshield is easier to repair than a large dent in the center of the hood."

"True." Jesse pulled his thoughts from the past to the present. "I just don't understand why anyone would want to seek vengeance by damaging my car."

Garth shot him a questioning glance. "And you're absolutely sure no one has an ax to grind? Maybe someone from work who knew you'd be here in town for your sister's wedding?"

He spread his hands wide. "Like who? The Albanians who attacked my most recent client's server with ransomware? I don't think so."

"Seems unlikely," Garth agreed. "Is it really Albanians who are behind the instances of ransomware? That's interesting."

"It's hard to know where the ransomware originates, but it's a known fact that both Albanians and Russians are experts at using the dark web."

"Wow, that's crazy. And you're the one who stops them, huh?"

"Sometimes." He'd once loved digging into computer software security systems to find their weaknesses, but lately he had been getting tired of the nonstop travel. "I mean, I try, but often it's a matter of skill combined with a bit of luck. Not to mention long hours of tedious work."

"I can see how that might get old. But some of the stories I've heard about ransomware are scary. They've taken on some big Fortune 500 companies."

"True." Jesse was bound by privacy agreements, most of the companies he worked for didn't want it known that their software had been infiltrated by ransomware. And not all ransomware was the same. Some just held the internal operating system hostage until a Bitcoin payment was made, but others were destructive viruses that took down the entire system even after the ransom was paid.

Computer terrorism was on the rise, no question about it. And his and Brian's company, Software Solutions, Inc., was poised to take advantage.

Garth pulled into the driveway of the McNallys' B&B. Jesse pushed open his door and climbed out of the police vehicle. "Thanks, Garth."

"No problem. Tell Jemma I'll see her around five."

"Sure." Jesse watched as his sister's fiancé turned around in the spacious parking lot and headed back into town.

The sounds of hammering could be heard coming from the apartment over the garage. He'd learned that the space was to provide Jemma and Trey a place to live that was still close enough to run the B&B, especially with intercom access so the guests could reach her if needed.

With time on his hands, now that he couldn't take a drive along the lakeshore, he headed to the apartment. Working with tools wasn't his specialty, but he was curious about the progress. Earlier, it had sounded like Jemma and Trey might be able to move in within the next few days.

The stairs leading up to the apartment were still rough, but once he'd cleared the landing, he paused, impressed by how great the place looked.

"Wow." He entered the kitchen area where Dalton was installing cabinets. "This is amazing."

"Yeah." Dalton grinned and swiped his forearm across his brow. The July sun shining through the open windows made the garage apartment unbearably warm. "Once these cabinets are finished, I'm working on installing the central air-conditioning and furnace units. They're the last things I need to complete before Jemma and Trey can move in."

Jesse nodded, sweeping his gaze over the open-concept kitchen and living room. The scent of fresh paint was strong. Crossing the area, he poked his head into the bathroom and the two bedrooms.

"Garth, Jemma, and Trey are going to be happy here," he said, turning back to Dalton. "You and Jazz did great."

"Trust me, others in the family provided a helping hand." Dalton tipped a glass of lemonade to his lips.

"What do you need me to do?" He felt compelled to make the offer. "I'm not mechanically inclined, but I can paint."

"Painting is finished. Really, we're all set. Jemma wants to move by Wednesday because that way you can stay in the master suite and they can rent the additional room for the weekend."

A wave of guilt hit hard. "My room? Why didn't she say something? I don't need the master suite. I can stay in a motel."

"Hey, that's a battle you need to have with your twin sisters, leave me out of it." Dalton picked up the heavy battery-powered screwdriver. "All I know is that Jemma wanted you to have the master suite because she has all six rooms rented for a weekend wedding."

"Yeah, sure." He couldn't argue the fact that his twin sisters had done such an outstanding job of making the McNallys' B&B a success. Still, he wished Jemma or Jazz had mentioned the fact that they needed the green room for a wedding when he'd asked to stay an extra week.

It felt as if people were keeping secrets from him, and he didn't like it. Carla Templeton's secret being the most infuriating of all.

So far, his idea of staying in McNally Bay for a mini-vacation was proving to be anything but relaxing.

CARLA COULDN'T KEEP her mind focused on all the tasks she needed to do for the grocery store. When she had to go through her list of items that needed to be restocked for the third time, she pushed the inventory aside and dropped her head into her hands.

She had no idea what to say to Jesse. Wished, really, that she didn't have to tell him anything at all. The guilt she'd lived with for the past nine years returned full force.

Jesse wouldn't forgive her for keeping Cassie's existence a secret. And sure, she knew it hadn't been fair to him or to her daughter. But Cassie was a normal, well-adjusted child, and Jesse had continued to study programming in college, while she'd been forced to drop out of the University of Iowa to return home. He'd flourished in his career, while she'd caused her father's heart attack and subsequent death, then lived with her mother and worked as a cashier at the grocery store while her mom ran the place in her dad's absence.

Not fair. Yet it had been her choice, one she'd never regret. She loved Cassie and couldn't imagine her life without her daughter. She massaged her temples. What did Jesse want? The question nagged at her. Did he really think he could waltz into her life, picking up with her as if the nine years between them hadn't happened?

As if she hadn't driven all the way up to Madison over homecoming weekend to tell him she was pregnant, only to find him kissing another woman?

Enough. Ruminating over the past was useless. The only thing that mattered was the here and now. She needed to find some way of convincing Jesse that the best thing for Cassie was for him to move on with his life, without telling her the truth.

It was about as likely to happen as snow in July, but she clung to the vain hope as she made it through the rest of her day.

Before heading to Gino's to meet Jesse, she stopped at home.

"Mom! Glad you're here." Cassie ran over to give her a welcoming hug. "I just finished walking Bucky. He's so much fun."

"I'm glad." She pasted a smile on her face as she returned Cassie's hug. For a moment, she wanted to cling to the little girl, to protect her from the harsh reality looming over their heads like a dark thundercloud. She pressed a kiss to the top of Cassie's head and met her mother's gaze. "Any problems?"

"No." Her mother's troubled expression was all she needed to know that Cassie had blabbed about how she'd met with her old friend Mr. Jesse. "I really think you should consider hiring an assistant manager for the store. Cassie is growing so fast; you're missing too much of your daughter's life working such long hours."

It was an ongoing argument, one she was weary of having. "I tried that, Mom, remember? Doris hadn't lasted a month. And the guy after that, Richard Knotts, hadn't made it through two weeks."

"Third time could be a charm," her mother pointed out.

"Maybe." But doubtful. McNally Bay wasn't a hotspot for the new generation. Most of the young adults were anxious to move to the city, either Chicago, Detroit, or Indianapolis. Somewhere they viewed as exciting. It had been her plan when she was young. Until she'd learned of her pregnancy. "Listen, I need to run out for a while. Would you mind putting Cassie to bed?"

"Not at all." Her mother glanced at Cassie, then pointedly at her. "I hear you're meeting up with your old boyfriend, Jesse McNally."

Her mother's comment felt like an arrow piercing her lung, stealing her breath. Was it possible her mother had guessed the truth? The night of her father's heart attack and sudden death were all too clear in her mind.

At the time, she'd denied Jesse was Cassie's father. She'd claimed it was someone she'd met at U of I. A guy who hadn't been interested in sticking around to be a father.

"Mr. Jesse was your boyfriend?" Cassie asked, her green eyes bright with interest.

Her heart gave a betraying thump as she remembered how it felt to be Jesse's girl. The song had been one of their favorites. Then she pulled herself together and shot a stern glare at her mother before responding. "No, honey. He's not my boyfriend. I hung around with him and his family one summer, that's all."

Thankfully, her mother didn't push the issue. "Well, have fun, dear. Don't worry about Cassie, we'll be fine."

"It's not a date." Carla wanted to scream the words at the top of her lungs, but she managed to maintain her composure. "He's only in town for a few days. Don't read anything more into this than there is."

"I won't, especially since the McNally men are known to be players. He's no good for you, Carla. But what about Mr. Thomas? There's no reason you can't have a little fun seeing someone," her mother protested. "You work too hard."

She needed to work hard if she wanted to prevent the store from going under. All the money they made during the busy tourist season had to be enough to sustain them over the long winter when visitors were as rare as an albino deer. It wasn't as if the store was in trouble, but it took a lot of energy and effort to keep it profitable.

"I'll be home within the hour." She gave Cassie another hug and kiss. "Be nice for Grandma, okay? I'll see you in the morning."

"Okay. G'night, Mom." Cassie didn't seem the least bit upset at her leaving.

As she walked outside to her ancient blue Honda Civic, she tried to ignore the overwhelming sense of dread. Telling herself that Jesse McNally would be reasonable about this wasn't working.

Tightening her grip on the steering wheel, she drove down Main Street to Gino's Pizzeria. It had once been their favorite hangout. And in the nine years since then, the place hadn't changed much. Locals and tourists alike flocked to the restaurant. The pizza was amazing. Gino Salvatore had immigrated from Italy many years ago and still owned the place. But he made it clear he wasn't about to share his special pizza sauce recipe with anyone.

She was fifteen minutes late but figured Jesse would wait. After all, this meeting was per his request, not hers. She parked in what looked to be the last parking spot in the small cramped lot. When she saw the large glossy red pickup truck, she recognized it as belonging to Jazz McNally, Jesse's younger sister.

Next to Jesse, Jazz was the one she'd missed the most from that infamous summer. But as the years passed, she'd stayed far away from the entire McNally clan. Not a difficult task until the past four months when Jemma and Jazz had decided to turn the old McNally Mansion into a B&B.

Steeling her resolve, she squared her shoulders and entered the restaurant. The place was packed with people, so she hovered near the doorway, sweeping her gaze over the occupants in an effort to find Jesse.

He wasn't there.

Was she mistaken about the red truck belonging to Jazz? She didn't think so, but with the amount of Chicago and Detroit tourists who flocked to the area in the summer months, she could be wrong.

A flicker of disappointment caught her off guard. Ridiculous. She was glad Jesse hadn't shown. Maybe he'd realized that Cassie was better off not knowing about him. He'd disrupt her life, and not in a good way since he wasn't staying.

No one stayed in McNally Bay for long.

Telling herself she was relieved he hadn't come, she turned and went back outside. As she approached her car, she heard a low moan.

The crime rate in the area was low, but not nonexistent. She dug in her purse for the can of pepper spray and cautiously stepped closer.

"I'm calling the cops," she said loudly, hoping to scare off whoever was hiding there.

The moan came again, louder this time. With a frown, she noticed a pair of jean-clad legs sticking out from the brush in front of the truck.

"Hey, are you all right?" She didn't want to get too close, in case this was nothing more than a clever trap.

A single mother couldn't be too careful.

There was no response, but she was beginning to believe that someone was hurt. Dropping the pepper spray back into her bag, she cautiously stepped closer.

It wasn't easy to see in the dusk, so she used her flashlight app and swept the beam over the supine figure. She gasped when she recognized the man lying in the dirt with his eyes closed and the side of his head covered in blood.

Jesse McNally.

3

———————

The sledgehammer in his head wouldn't stop, the pain reverberating with every beat of his heart. For a moment, he couldn't remember what happened. Upon hearing a female voice talking to him, he did his best to focus on what she was saying.

"Jesse? I'm calling an ambulance."

"No. I'm fine." He blinked and put up a hand to shield the light shining on him. "Carla?"

"You're hurt, may even have a concussion." The light moved away from his face, and he could make out Carla's worried expression as she knelt beside him.

"Just—um—give me a minute." He pushed himself up on his elbows, swallowing a groan as the pain in his head intensified. If he said too much about how awful he felt, she'd call the ambulance for sure.

"What happened?" Carla's voice was full of concern, and he found it ironic that it took being hit on the side of his head for her to stop being angry with him. At least, temporarily.

"I got out of the truck and felt someone come up alongside me. I thought it was you, but then something hit me hard on the side of the head."

"I promise it wasn't me." Carla's voice held a note of uncertainty as if she was upset that he'd believed she was the one who'd hit him. "I was late because I stopped at home after work to see Cassie before she went to bed. I went inside Gino's and, when I didn't see you, came back out here."

"I know it wasn't you." No matter how upset Carla might feel toward him for reasons he still didn't understand, he couldn't imagine her resorting to physical violence. Besides, this recent attack had to be related to the brick through his windshield.

But who in McNally Bay hated him this much? He'd only been in town for a few days, and until today, most of that time had been spent with his family.

"We should call the police," Carla said. "You need to report this."

It made sense, but he felt as if it would be a futile effort. How would the sheriff's deputies figure out who'd attacked him? Especially since he had no idea who was holding a grudge?

"Fine." He swiped the blood from his face with the hem of his T-shirt, then reached out toward her. "Help me up, would you?"

There was a slight hesitation before she reached out to take his hand. Her slender hand was warm, yet firm. With her support, he managed to stagger to his feet. His stomach rolled with nausea, but he forced himself to ignore it. "Thanks."

"I'm calling the cops." Carla dropped his hand as if she'd been burned, then dug out her phone. As she dialed the 911 dispatcher, he tried to remember if he'd noticed anyone lurking nearby prior to being smacked.

Unfortunately, he hadn't been paying attention to his surroundings, too focused on the upcoming discussion with Carla about Cassie.

"They're sending a deputy." Carla gestured to her car. "Maybe you should sit down."

She was right, he wasn't feeling great. She opened the passenger side door of her car, and he gratefully lowered himself down on the seat. When she moved away, he frowned. "Hold on, we still need to talk."

"I know." She turned to face him, her expression guarded. "But we should wait until you've been checked out."

Jesse felt the opportunity might disappear forever if they didn't hash things out here and now. "Just tell me the truth. Is Cassie my daughter?"

She stared at him for a long moment before slowly nodding. "Yes. But if you want what's best for her, you'll keep this information to yourself. No one else needs to know."

Hearing her say the words he'd expected didn't lessen the impact. He could only focus on one issue at a time. "I don't understand. Why didn't you tell me?"

"I drove up to Madison to do just that, but you were—otherwise occupied. With a blonde."

Otherwise occupied with a blonde? He felt as if she'd hit him with another brick. "What are you talking about?"

She let out her breath in a heavy sigh. "I saw you, Jesse. Kissing the blonde. Or don't you remember we discussed getting together that weekend?"

A flash of guilt hit hard.

"Yeah, not only did you forget you invited me, but I found you with the blonde. So I left."

For the life of him, he couldn't remember a blonde, but he did remember discussing how they'd get together. "When?"

"Homecoming weekend." She shrugged and looked away. "I know it was always party-town in Madison during homecoming, but frankly I was preoccupied with the fact that I'd just learned I was pregnant."

Oh man. He'd blown it big time. His plans with Carla hadn't ever been finalized, but he had mentioned getting together over homecoming weekend. Thinking back now, he vaguely remembered being with a large group of freshmen during homecoming. They'd had a fair amount to drink, so the memories were blurry. Had he been kissing a blonde? Maybe. But it wasn't long after that weekend that he turned his back on the party scene to focus on his grades. He'd been offered a scholarship to attend the university, and payments were dependent on his maintaining a good GPA.

"Look, Carla, I'm sorry. You're right, I had mentioned getting together, but we never really made final plans. And I . . . had a little too much fun that weekend, but if I had known you were there, that you needed me, I would have acted differently."

Her expression was full of doubt. "Yeah, I'm sure."

He squelched a flash of anger. "Did it occur to you to try calling first? If I had known you were coming, I wouldn't have been out with my friends. Come on, Carla, you have to know that I'm not the kind of guy who would turn his back on his responsibilities."

Before she could answer, a brown Clark County Sheriff's Deputy squad rolled into Gino's parking lot. Carla moved away, flagging the deputy over. A pretty woman slid out from behind the wheel, and Jesse nodded in greeting.

"I'm Deputy Waldorf. What happened here?"

"I'm Carla Templeton, and this is Jesse McNally. I found him lying unconscious in the bushes."

"McNally?" Deputy Waldorf echoed. "Related to Jemma and Jazz, right?"

"Yeah. I'm one of the older brothers." He was used to being known as just one of the McNally boys, his oldest brother Jake had been a bit on the wild side, which meant that the rest of them had been treated the same way. Jeremy was second oldest, then him, then Jonas, and finally the twins, Jemma and Jazz.

With a wince, he understood that no matter what stunts Jake and Jeremy had pulled, Jesse was the one who'd fathered an illegitimate child. To his knowledge, no one else in the family had done anything like that.

It was something everyone would expect of Jake, not him.

"Why don't you start at the beginning?" Deputy Waldorf suggested.

Jesse repeated the brief narrative, keeping out the part about how he hadn't been paying attention because he'd been thinking about the daughter he'd just met earlier that day. Deputy Waldorf tried to convince him to be checked out by an ambulance, but he refused.

"I feel just like the time I was hit by the two-ton linebacker while playing high school football. I'll be fine."

"And you're sure you have no idea who might be holding a grudge against you?"

He glanced at Carla, who was standing off to the side, her arms crossed protectively over his chest, before responding. "I'm sure. I've only been here since Friday.

Four days doesn't seem long enough to make local enemies."

"There are plenty of tourists," Carla pointed out. "For all you know, someone could have followed you here."

"That's true," Deputy Waldorf echoed thoughtfully. "What did you say your job entailed?"

"I'm a computer geek." It was the easiest way to describe it. "I investigate and restore computer security systems of companies that have been hacked."

"Hmm." Deputy Waldorf's tone was noncommittal.

"Exactly," Jesse said on a sigh. "Not exactly the type of job that creates enemies."

"I would still recommend that you make a list of your former clients. Could be that someone feels you didn't do a very good job."

"Maybe." He wasn't going to agree to any such thing, primarily because of the confidentiality agreements he'd signed. But it may be worth the effort of calling his partner, Brian Malone. Their company was very successful, and if there was the possibility of a client holding a grudge, his partner needed to know.

Avery and Arch in particular hadn't been thrilled with the length of time their system was down. But he had eventually restored it. Surely they couldn't be upset about that?

"Call me when you have that list." Deputy Waldorf closed her small notebook and tucked it into her pocket. "Or if you remember anything else that may help us find the person responsible."

"No video cameras?" He looked up at Gino's building.

"No." Deputy Waldorf lifted a brow. "This is McNally Bay, not Chicago."

He understood what she was saying. The quaint town was a nice vacation spot but hardly functioned the way big cities did, with video cameras on every stop-and-go light and on top of various buildings.

After the deputy left, Carla eyed him warily. He could tell she wanted him out of her car, but he didn't move.

"Listen, Jesse, I need to go, but I'm happy to drive you home."

"Not yet. We still have a lot to talk about. I want to know all about Cassie. And I want to know when we can tell her that I'm her father."

Carla's expression turned grim. "We aren't telling her anything. Why would you want to disrupt her life like that? She's eight. Not old enough to understand why you showed up now out of the blue. And besides, it's not as if you're going to be around for long. You live in Chicago and your job involves a lot of travel, doesn't it?"

How did she know that? Had she been secretly following him all these years? He mainly used social media to keep in touch with his siblings, without posting a lot about his personal life.

He tried to pull his thoughts together. "Carla, she's my daughter. A McNally. I want to be a part of her life."

"A part-time father?" Carla let out a harsh laugh. "Why am I not surprised? I'm sure that will work for a year at the most, and then those visits will get less and less until they're nonexistent, leaving Cassie to wonder what she did to make you mad."

That made him wince. "That's not what I meant. Yes, my job involves travel, but I can control my schedule to a certain degree. I can decline jobs that are too far away. And I would never make Cassie feel bad."

"And live here in McNally Bay between jobs?"

His initial instinct was to agree, but he knew it wasn't practical. Living in Chicago, close to a large airport, was important. Traveling in and out of McNally Bay would take far too long. He wasn't even sure where the closest airport was from here. Kalamazoo? Maybe.

He tried to think of a compromise, but his brain was still feeling a bit scrambled.

"Yeah, that's what I thought." Carla gave an impatient wave. "Do you want a lift home or not?"

He pushed himself upright, closing the passenger side door behind him. "No, I'm fine, but I'd rather keep talking for a while. I still have questions. I'd like to hear everything about Cassie. What she likes, how school is going, what are her favorite pastimes..."

"Sorry, but I don't have time for this. I need to be at work early in the morning." Carla pulled out her keys and opened the driver's side door. "Goodbye, Jesse."

It wasn't goodbye, but he didn't prevent her from leaving, standing and watching long after the red taillights were no longer visible.

The issues Carla had brought up were important. Big questions and concerns he needed time to digest. Up until now, he'd been more upset at the fact that she'd kept Cassie a secret all these years than worrying about how they'd interact in the future.

As much as he wanted to be a part of his daughter's life, he knew he needed time to regroup. To figure out how to make that work.

But no way was this over. Not by a long shot.

He wasn't giving up his daughter that easily.

CARLA DROVE AWAY from Gino's with a knot in her stomach. She should be happy she'd won the first round, but she sensed that, for Jesse, the issue wasn't even close to being resolved.

The Jesse she remembered was stubborn and tenacious. When she'd thrown what was best for Cassie at him, he'd surprised her by appearing to consider her point.

Logically, she knew he wouldn't do anything to hurt Cassie. But he didn't understand the complicated relationship between a father and a daughter.

Her relationship with her father wasn't a good example either. Her father had treated her indifferently as if he couldn't care where she was or what she was doing. She'd envied her friends who had fathers who doted on them.

She didn't want to remember the last week of her father's life. The sting of his hand against her face. The burning humiliation, which had been so much worse than the physical pain. The anger and disappointment in his eyes. The way he'd scathingly told her the father of her baby better not be one of those *no-good McNallys*.

It was the most difficult time of her life. Worse, really, than driving up to Madison, Wisconsin, to find Jesse kissing a beautiful blonde. The two events back-to-back had sent her reeling into a deep pit of guilt. Still, nine years later and she didn't understand what her father had meant by *those no-good McNallys*. She'd tried to ask her mother about the animosity that her father had toward the McNally family, but her mother had refused to talk about it.

And Carla hadn't pushed. Because after her father's death, it was all she could do to keep her mother from sliding into a pit of despair. Being pregnant with the first and only grandchild had certainly been a distraction. They'd stayed focused on preparing Cassie's room and all the items she'd need once Carla brought Cassie home.

There hadn't been a baby shower, so they'd scrimped

and saved buying a little bit each month until they had everything ready.

Because she owed her mother so much, especially with all the childcare she'd provided, Carla hadn't wanted to do anything to rock the boat. But now, she couldn't stop wondering about her father's reaction. Sure, any man would be upset to learn his eighteen-year-old daughter was pregnant, but why hold a grudge specifically against the McNallys?

She'd taken full responsibility for her mistakes. And Cassie was a blessing. Her daughter was so full of life, of joy that she didn't regret a single minute.

And she had never forgotten what it felt like to be held in Jesse's strong arms.

The drive to the home she shared with her mother and daughter didn't take long. It was close enough to the store that she walked to work each morning as a way to save on wear and tear on her ancient vehicle. While she was doing fine financially, she wasn't extravagant by nature.

No little red Corvette, that's for sure.

Shaking her head at her foolishness, she parked in the driveway and slid out from behind the wheel. As she approached the front door, she heard her name.

"Carla?"

She spun toward the sound, putting a hand up to cover her racing heart. A man of average height and weight approached from the street, and she frowned, wondering why she hadn't seen him when she pulled in. It took her a moment to recognize Dean Thomas, the principal of Cassie's school.

"Sorry, didn't mean to scare you," Dean said. "I came by earlier, but your mom said you were out."

"You waited for me?" Despite the warm summer air, she felt a chill. "Why?"

"Oh no, not really." Dean's brown hair was already thinning on top, despite the fact that he was only about eight years her senior. He cleared his throat and shuffled his feet as if sensing her distress. "I was down on Main Street when I saw you drive by." He shrugged and smiled. "I decided to head over."

Their house was just one block off Main Street, but his story didn't quite make sense. She should have seen him walking toward her house.

Then again, she had been lost in the past. Reliving those distressing early days when she'd found out she was pregnant with Jesse's child.

"Okay, uh, did you need something?" She finally broke the tense silence. "It's getting late. I have to open the store at eight o'clock tomorrow morning."

"Oh, nothing urgent." Dean shoved his hands into the pockets of his tan slacks. "I wanted to invite you to have dinner with me on Saturday night."

She did her best to hide her discomfort. Dean was a nice guy, but she had zero interest in dating him. The coffee they'd shared had been an uncomfortable and stilted experience. One she didn't care to repeat.

An image of Jesse's adorable grin, so much like Cassie's, flashed in her mind. "Dean, I'm so sorry, but I'm not interested in dating anyone right now. Truly, it's all I can do to manage my responsibilities at the store and with Cassie." She smiled in an effort to take the sting out of her rejection. "You're a great guy, and you deserve someone special."

"And that's not you." His words were flat, and she nearly winced.

"I'm sorry," she repeated, wishing more than anything

she'd given Jesse a ride home. Anything to avoid this awkward interaction with the principal of her daughter's school. She hoped he wouldn't take his frustration regarding her lack of interest in him out on her daughter.

Cassie was a good kid, yet far from perfect. She'd gotten into trouble when she'd punched a boy for calling her names. Cassie hadn't hit him hard enough to bruise, but the boy's mother had gone crazy demanding Cassie be expelled. Principal Thomas had stood up for Cassie, and she'd been grateful for his support.

"Yeah, me, too." Dean Thomas stared at her for a long moment, before turning and retracing his steps.

Relief washed over her once he disappeared from sight. Hopefully, that was the end of it.

But it wasn't until later that it occurred to her that if Dean Thomas was on Main Street, then he could have seen her and Jesse talking together outside Gino's.

Was that the reason he'd dropped by to ask her out? Because of some weird sort of jealousy?

If so, brushing him off like that probably only made things worse.

4

———

When Jesse woke up the following morning in the green room of the B&B, his headache was better. Not gone, but better. He followed the scent of coffee down to the dining room where he found the place mostly empty except for a young couple seated at one of the tables overlooking the lakefront. Were they scoping the place out as a potential wedding site? Maybe.

Jazz came out of the kitchen carrying a pot of coffee. Her gaze brightened when she saw him, but then she frowned. "Jesse! What happened?"

Lifting a hand, he gingerly touched his bruised and swollen temple. "Some sort of weird welcome back to McNally Bay."

She filled his coffee mug, then leaned down to examine the wound more closely. "Someone attacked you? Why?"

"No clue." He gratefully took a sip of coffee. "Happened outside Gino's."

"Did you tell Garth?"

"I spoke with a Deputy Waldorf." There was no point in rehashing the fact that he had an enemy somewhere in town. "Would you tell Jemma I'd like the full Irish breakfast?"

"Sure." Jazz's expression was still troubled. "But I don't like this, Jesse. First your car, now this? What's next?"

It belatedly occurred to him that Jazz was concerned about something happening at the B&B. "Don't worry, I'll move to a motel first thing today. That way Jemma doesn't have to rush to take over the garage apartment."

Jazz waved that off. "She and Trey are dying to get their things up there, so don't think that you going to a motel will change that. Besides, it's the Fourth of July weekend, you won't find a place to stay at the last minute. Lastly, and I can't stress this enough, we like having you here."

He was touched by her comments but knew that staying here may bring the danger dogging his footsteps to their door. And that was not acceptable.

Jazz went over to chat with the young couple before disappearing into the kitchen. She emerged less than five minutes later with a warm-from-the-oven blueberry muffin and slice of chocolate zucchini bread. "Enjoy."

The zucchini bread and muffin were equally delicious. He had to hand it to Jemma, she was one amazing cook. He'd checked their website when he'd first arrived in town, making a few adjustments for them, but he had been impressed by the rave reviews posted online about the McNallys' B&B.

The twins were doing a great job running the place. And offering the gazebo wedding package was pure genius.

The young couple left just as Jazz brought his breakfast. He gestured to the seat across from him. "Join me for a minute, would you? I have a few questions about the Tate-McNally family feud."

Jazz grimaced and sat. "Don't tell me you've had a run-in with Leon Tate already."

"Not exactly a run-in, but he was gloating over my damaged car outside Daisy's." He paused for a moment to try his breakfast before continuing. "Garth mentioned that Leon and his daughter Mary are holding some lifelong grudge against us because of something Dad did a million years ago."

"That's true." Jazz hesitated and glanced at her watch. "Listen, let me give Jemma a hand in the kitchen, then we'll both fill you in on what's been going on."

He nodded and continued eating. It was almost five minutes before both Jemma and Jazz came out of the kitchen to join him. Jemma brought a cup of tea with her, while Jazz helped herself to coffee. Jazz pulled out a slip of paper and set it on the table next to his plate.

"Here's what we know so far," she began. "We knew from day one of returning here that Leon Tate hated us. He made that perfectly clear, gloating over the vandalism here at the B and B the same way he did over your ruined Corvette. Jemma found this letter in the attic addressed to a girl named Lucy and signed J."

"Not helpful to sign with only a first initial," he pointed out. "The McNallys went nuts on the J names."

"Right? But you'll see it's more recent than from our grandparents' era."

Intrigued, Jesse leaned forward to read the letter.

Dearest Lucy,

My world is dark without you in it. I don't understand how this happened, and I'm finding it difficult to move on without you.

Life is so precious yet so brief. In one fleeting moment it's gone, as if it had never been. I've searched the Bible for answers but have found no solace to ease my pain. Some would say I haven't tried hard enough, and that may be true. It isn't easy to dissect one's mistakes, holding them up to the glaring light of day.

This suffering is my price to pay.

Always, J.

"Wow." Jesse glanced at the twins. "You think Dad wrote this? And who is Lucy?"

"I'm afraid so." Jemma's expression was sad. "Jonas and Bella went to the library to find more information about Lucy and uncovered that her last name was Tate and that she was Leon's younger sister. She died when she was sixteen years old."

Understanding dawned. "And Leon blames our dad for his sister's death."

"Yes, because he was driving the speedboat when she fell into Lake Michigan and drowned." Jazz picked up the story. "And worse, we heard a rumor that the Medical Examiner found a bruise on Lucy's temple that was likely suffered prior to the drowning."

He whistled. "That's not good."

"No," Jazz agreed. "There were three other guys on the boat that night, so four boys and one girl. Dad was driving the boat, but we think it's likely that there was some sort of argument between the other three boys and Lucy, which resulted in her being struck and ultimately contributed to her death."

He glanced between Jemma and Jazz. "But no one was arrested?"

"Exactly." Jemma sipped her tea. "All four boys stuck to the same story, the details of which we don't know. Regardless, Leon has made it clear our father is responsible for his younger sister's death."

"But that doesn't make sense, he's the one least likely to be involved," Jesse pointed out. "He was driving the boat."

"And dating Lucy," Jazz added. She gestured to the note. "Apparently they were in love, and that was the reason Lucy was on the boat in the first place."

In a warped way, it made sense. Not entirely logical, but emotions rarely were. One of the reasons he liked computer work was because it was cut-and-dried. Black-and-white. No in-between.

"Mystery solved." He stared down at the letter, wondering what his father would say about that night if he was still alive. Unfortunately, his dad's secret died with him.

"Not exactly," Jazz said. "We don't know the true story. Personally, I'd like to know who the other boys were on the boat that night. We may be able to learn the truth, which may in turn help put Leon Tate's animosity to rest."

"Doubtful." Jesse wasn't convinced. "I mean, sure, we might be able to find out who the other three boys were on the boat that night, but if they've kept this a secret for all these years, why talk now?"

Jemma frowned. "To clear their conscience?"

He shook his head. "Not happening. But at least I understand why Leon was smirking at my damaged car. Maybe I need to convince Garth to look closer at Leon and his daughter. Could be their anger is escalating."

"Maybe." Jazz's expression held doubt. "Although it doesn't make sense that anger would be directed at you when Jemma and I are the ones living here in McNally Bay full time. Anyway, if you have some free time, we'd love your help in getting Jemma's stuff moved to the garage apartment."

"Happy to help. But then I'm moving into a motel."

"Oh, please don't." Jemma's expression displayed her disappointment. "We really want you to stay."

It was difficult to say no to his sisters. And if it wasn't for Cassie, he'd pack up and head home. "One more day," he promised. "But if something else happens, I'm out of here."

"Nothing more is going to happen." Jemma sounded confident, but he didn't believe it.

After he assisted with moving Jemma's things, he cleared his stuff out of the green room and into the master suite. Then he decided to head down to the sheriff's deputy head-quarters. There had to be a way to uncover who was responsible for these two events.

He wanted things to be cleared up as soon as possible so he could focus his time and energy on Carla and Cassie Templeton.

Carla headed to the grocery store, inwardly debating whether or not she should call Deputy Waldorf to let her know about how Dean Thomas had shown up at her house last night, within twenty minutes of Jesse's attack. It didn't make sense that the principal of Cassie's school would do anything to hurt Jesse, but the timing was odd.

Could be nothing more than a coincidence. Sure, Dean may have seen her and Jesse talking, but it wasn't as if they'd embraced or shown any display of being close. And they'd spoken after the attack, not before.

Yet the impending sense of doom wouldn't leave her alone. She knew it was only a matter of time until the entire town of McNally Bay knew the truth. Seeing Jesse at the diner had reinforced the resemblance between him and their daughter. Especially their mannerisms and facial expressions.

She needed to talk to Cassie before the gossipmongers like Betty Cromwell blabbed the news to anyone who would listen.

Tonight. She'd talk to Cassie tonight, after she was finished with work. It wouldn't be easy, but she hoped her daughter would forgive her.

And that Cassie's relationship with her father would turn out better than hers had been.

The moment she entered the store, she was bombarded with problems. A food shipment hadn't arrived as promised, their stock of Fourth of July sparklers was already gone, with two days before the holiday, and her early morning cashier was a no-show for work.

In times like this, having an assistant manager would be helpful, but dreaming about what couldn't be wasn't going to get her through the day.

By lunchtime, Carla felt as if she'd worked twelve hours instead of four. Despite her exhaustion, she headed over to Daisy's Diner to have lunch with Cassie.

She desperately wished she could spend more time with her daughter, especially during the summer months when Cass was out of school. Her little girl was growing so fast. She wanted to hold back the hands of time, already dreading the upcoming teenage rebellion she was certain loomed on the horizon.

Cassie was outside the back of the diner, playing with Bucky, Daisy's Goldendoodle puppy. Just watching them together, the sheer joy in her daughter's carefree laughter, made her heart ache.

This was what was important. For the first time, she wondered what her mother would think if she sold the grocery store. But if she did that, she'd need to find another job.

"Mom! Isn't Bucky amazing?"

Carla nodded. As she approached, the Goldendoodle pup came rushing over, jumping up and down with excitement. "Get down," she admonished.

Bucky's entire body wiggled with happiness as she scratched him behind the ears. The puppy was growing like a weed, and she knew he'd be a good eighty pounds by the time he was a year old.

"Is the dog yours, Cassie?"

The familiar male voice had Carla spinning around to face Jesse. The bruise on his temple didn't look any better in the harsh sunlight, but any sympathy she may have had toward him evaporated at his unwelcome intrusion on their mother/daughter time. He didn't seem fazed by the glare she sent him, his attention centered on their daughter.

"Not mine, Mr. Jesse. Bucky belongs to Miss Daisy. But I'm helping her take care of Bucky while she works."

"I see." Jesse's smile was so much like Cassie's she wanted to cry.

"Why don't you put Bucky in his crate?" she suggested. "I know Miss Daisy is saving us a seat inside."

"Okay. Bye, Mr. Jesse." For once, Cassie did as she was told, taking the rambunctious Bucky inside the diner to put the dog in his kennel.

"What are you doing here?" The instant her daughter was out of earshot she whirled on him. "I thought we settled this issue last night?"

"We didn't," Jesse corrected. "You told me your opinion and then left without giving me a chance to respond."

"Really? Does that mean you've decided to move to

McNally Bay?" She wanted to smack some sense into him. Why was he being so stubborn about this?

"There are other arrangements we can make," he countered. "I can come here to visit between jobs, and she can come and stay with me during some weekends where she might not have school."

"No." The very idea of handing Jesse partial custody of their daughter made her break out in a cold sweat. "Cassie doesn't even know you, what makes you think she's going to feel comfortable spending weekends with you? Especially in a strange place far away from her friends?"

"And whose fault is that?" He looked at her, and for the first time, she saw the stirring of anger in the depths of his eyes. "You could have called me, Carla."

This wasn't the time or the place to rehash the mistakes of the past. Or to explain how her own father had reacted to the news. Announcing her pregnancy had caused her father to suffer a heart attack that had killed him.

At eighteen, knowing she'd hurt her father while dealing with her pregnancy was about all she could handle.

"Not now," she hissed as Cassie returned.

Jesse didn't reply, but he didn't back off either.

"Miss Daisy has a table for us," Cassie announced. "She said to tell you to hurry because the diner is filling up fast."

"May I join you?"

Jesse's soft question caught her off guard, despite the fact that she probably should have expected it. She wanted to refuse, but he'd asked in front of Cassie who watched the interaction between the adults with blatant curiosity.

"Sure." Feeling trapped, she relented. But if he so much as broached the topic of being Cassie's father, she'd ruthlessly cut him off at the knees.

"I'm going to try the fried chicken today," Cassie said as

they headed inside through the back door. The locals liked to stick together, and Daisy had pretty much adopted Cassie over the years. Hence the saving of a table for their daily lunches.

"Is that your favorite?" Jesse asked, holding the door for them.

"I have lots of favorites," Cass confided as they went inside. "Miss Daisy's fried chicken is just one of them. I like her apple pie, too. And her pork chops are yummy."

To his credit, Jesse hung on Cassie's words, soaking up every morsel of information she doled out. The way he looked at Cassie with love and adoration made her remember how he'd once looked at her the same way.

It hurt to remember how much she'd loved him.

"What are your favorite subjects in school?" he asked after Ashley took their order.

"Not math. I hate math." Cassie wrinkled her nose at the thought of arithmetic and multiplication tables. "Reading and writing are my favorites. I want to be a writer someday."

"You do?" Carla hadn't said much during the conversation between Jesse and their daughter until now. "I didn't know that."

"My teacher told me I have a good voice for telling stories," Cassie confided. "Grandma takes me to the library every day because I read so fast."

"I knew you liked to read," she responded dryly. "I just didn't know you wanted to be a writer someday."

"Grandma told me I should take a job at the store with you because it's hard being a starving artist." Cassie wrinkled her brow. "I don't get it. What does being a starving artist have to do with writing books?"

"It means that making money isn't always easy to do when you are painting or writing or doing some other form of art," Carla explained. "You only make money if people buy what you've produced. If they don't buy your items, you'll starve."

"But everyone likes books," Cassie protested.

She had to smile. "I wish that was true, but not everyone enjoys reading the way we do."

"You work at the grocery store?" Jesse asked as Ashley brought their food in what seemed like record time.

"Mommy is the general manager of the store," Cassie said proudly. She took a bite of her fried chicken, then added, "Our family has owned the store for three generations, right, Mom?"

"That's right." She could tell by the look of surprise on Jesse's face that he hadn't realized she'd dropped out of school. Idiot. Did he think she could attend U of I full time while caring for a baby? Yeah, not.

Before she could say anything more, Mrs. Cromwell approached. "Look at how sweet you all look together, one big happy family."

Family? Her panicked gaze cut to Jesse who looked just as stunned by Betty Cromwell's words.

"We're not a family," Cassie piped up. "Mr. Jesse was a friend of my mom from a long time ago."

"I know that, dear," Betty said, patting Cassie's arm. "I remember how smitten these two were back then."

Smitten? No. Oh, no. She knew. Betty Cromwell had put the two pieces of the puzzle together and came up with the truth.

The little time she thought she'd have had just run out. She and Cassie needed to talk. Now.

And as much as she knew that Cassie deserved to know who her father was, Carla was very much afraid that the light in her daughter's eyes would fade when she realized Carla hadn't been truthful with her over the past eight years.

Whoever said the truth will set you free was full of baloney.

In this case, the truth would only hurt the people she loved the most.

Cassie and her mother.

5

Carla's eyes filled with distress, so Jesse quickly put a hand on Mrs. Cromwell's arm. "Thanks for stopping by, but we only have a short time before Carla needs to get back to work, and I don't want our food to get cold. Would you mind giving us some time alone?"

"Oh sure, dear." The woman had the audacity to wink at him before moving on. "Henry! Over here!" She waved a hand at Mayor Henry Banks, indicating he should join her. He'd heard during the wedding that the burgeoning romance between Henry Banks and Betty Cromwell was the talk of the town.

Jesse wished the nosy woman would focus more on her own love life, and leave them alone. But it was clear that Betty had guessed he was Cassie's father, and that didn't bode well for them. The woman couldn't keep a secret if her life depended on it.

"Jesse, do you have time to stop by the house later?" Carla's tight smile didn't reach her eyes, the green gaze he'd fallen for the first time he'd met her that summer nine years ago.

"Of course." He understood she wanted to tell Cassie the truth and maybe needed some moral support. "But you know, it's a beautiful day out, we can take a drive along the lakeshore. Maybe sit overlooking the lake for a while."

"I have to work. The store doesn't close until eight o'clock tonight." Carla's tone was clipped as if she was annoyed by his offer.

"Mom always has to work," Cassie piped up. "She has lots of responsibilities."

"I know you're in charge, but I'm sure you could get away for a few hours." He wasn't sure why he was pushing so hard, other than he didn't like the idea of Carla working such long days. Did she really work twelve hours a day seven days a week? Totally crazy.

Besides, the conversation with Cassie couldn't wait. He had no doubt that Betty was already telling Mayor Banks all about it. The news would be rippling through town by dinnertime. "You must have people at the store you can trust to watch things in your absence."

Carla narrowed her gaze for a moment, then concentrated on eating her meal. He tried to think of a way to convince her to spend a few hours with him, but he wasn't sure how.

The confident, driven woman seated across from him was different from the carefree teenager he'd once loved.

"Please," he finally said in a low voice.

Carla finished her salad and pushed her plate away with a sigh. "All right, but it's been a crazy morning. I need an hour to make sure things are settled at the store."

"Thank you." He smiled and was glad when she managed to smile back. His gaze lingered on her face, his stomach tightening with awareness. How was it possible that Carla was more beautiful to him now than ever before?

They were both nine years older, but time had only made her more attractive. He couldn't help feeling guilty for how he'd allowed their relationship to get so intimate back in the summer after high school graduation.

He'd been weak, and Carla hadn't said no. But looking back, he couldn't deny he should have acted better. Been stronger. Done what was right.

His gaze shifted to Cassie, who was adorably licking her fingers after devouring her fried chicken. From the brief time he'd spent with her, he found her to be an amazing kid.

One he wasn't sure he could bear to leave, once his week of vacation time was up. His partner, Brian, had called yesterday asking when he'd be back and mentioning how Avery and Arch had finally paid their balance of the fee, while still grumbling about the time it had taken Jesse to do the job. At the end of the conversation, Brian claimed they had a new client demanding Jesse's expertise. Jesse had declined the job, insisting Brian should handle it himself.

"So, I'll see you in an hour?" Carla's voice interrupted his thoughts.

"Yes. An hour." He finished his fried chicken, having enjoyed eating Cassie's favorite, then gestured for the check. Ashley dropped the tab next to him, and he had to grab it quickly as Carla tried to reach for it.

"I'll pay our share," she said, digging in her purse.

"My treat. I invited myself to join you, remember?" It was the least he could do since he hadn't paid a dime of child support. And he fully intended to work out a financial arrangement moving forward. His job provided an excellent salary; he wanted to help Carla and Cassie. Maybe with decent child support coming in Carla wouldn't have to work such long hours.

"See you later, Mr. Jesse." Cassie favored him with a little wave as she and her mother left the diner.

Carla hadn't said much, and he knew the upcoming conversation must be weighing on her. He squelched a flash of annoyance that she'd kept Cassie a secret all these years. If he were honest, he'd admit that the phone calls that had slowly trickled off between them were his fault, more than hers. He'd been the one to mention she should come up to spend homecoming with him, but then he had never finalized any plans. It made him feel sick that Carla had come up anyway, only to find him with another girl.

He should have continued to follow up with her after that weekend, but he'd gotten so involved in life on campus that he'd never made the effort. When he hadn't heard from her, he'd figured she'd moved on and had done the same.

If he had reached out to her, he felt certain she would have told him about her pregnancy. His being in the dark was as much his fault as it was hers.

As he left the diner, his cell phone rang. Looking at the screen, he inwardly groaned when he saw the caller was Brian. He was tempted to let it go to voice mail, but he knew he'd only call again later.

"Hey, Brian," he said by way of greeting.

"Jesse, listen, I really need you for this new job. It's over my head."

"Since when?" Jesse was irritated with his old college roommate. "You and I both graduated with the same degree, right? You take on jobs like this every day."

"Okay, yes, I do, but this one is different." There was a nervous edge to Brian's tone, and Jesse wondered if he was having other, personal problems that were distracting him. "Please, Jesse, I need you on this. How soon can you get to Indianapolis?"

"If I leave Sunday when my week off is finished, I can be at the company first thing Monday morning."

"But today is only Tuesday! That's too long!"

"I haven't taken a week of vacation in over a year. I think I'm due." Jesse wasn't budging on this. Not when he needed to spend this time with his daughter.

And after the week was up? the voice in the back of his mind taunted him. He'd have to find a way to make it work. Even if that meant traveling from McNally Bay rather than Chicago. He'd done a bit of research earlier today and learned that both Kalamazoo and Grand Rapids had decent-sized airports. Not as big as Chicago, but not catering only to puddle jumpers either.

"Fine. I'll send the job elsewhere," Brian said in a curt tone.

Was his partner bluffing? He almost caved, then decided it didn't matter if his partner sent the job elsewhere. There would be another one to replace it soon enough. Their talent for being security experts was well known in the information technology community. And the hackers creating viruses and ransomware never seemed to take time off.

"Okay, see you next week." Jesse disconnected from the call before Brian could say anything more.

He didn't linger at the diner as people were already lining up at the door waiting for a table. He decided to walk down Main Street. The place was super busy with tourists, and he found himself wondering what it was like in the middle of winter. He knew from experience that Lake Michigan often froze solid during the long winter months, and he suspected the tourism was likely nonexistent outside of a few cross-country skiers and the like.

Did the lack of tourism impact Carla's grocery store?

Sure, the locals needed food and supplies, but was that enough to pay the bills? He made a mental note to ask Carla later.

After leaving the busy street, he turned and headed down toward the lakefront. There was something mesmerizing about watching the water. There were boats for rent, and he thought it would be great to take Carla and Cassie out for a ride.

He was lost in his thoughts, coming back to the present when the loud rumble of a motorcycle engine caught his attention. Jesse moved over to the side of the road to give the guy room.

The motorcycle driver stayed close. As he turned to frown at the guy, a fist lashed out, hitting Jesse hard in the shoulder as he drove by.

Knocked off balance, he hit the ground with a thud while trying to keep his gaze on the license plate. But it was no use. The small plate on the back of the motorcycle was covered with mud.

The driver took off, weaving in and out of traffic, disappearing from view before he could get his phone out to call the sheriff's department.

This was the third attack on him in two days, and he was getting mighty tired of being pushed around. And still, he couldn't figure out why in the world anyone in McNally Bay wanted to hurt him.

~

CARLA MANAGED to solve most of the problems at the store to the point she felt as if she should be able to be gone for two hours. She took her most senior cashier, Sheryl Watts, aside and explained that she was temporarily in charge, but if anything serious came up, she could be reached via her cell phone.

"I'll be fine," Sheryl assured her. "The next delivery isn't expected until four o'clock this afternoon. That gives you a couple of hours to relax and have fun."

Telling Cassie about Jesse McNally would hardly be relaxing or fun, but she didn't point that out. The news would be broadcast around all of Clark County soon enough.

Carla found herself wishing she was wearing something nicer than her traditional tan slacks and light blue polo shirt with the Templeton Grocery logo displayed above the right breast. But there wasn't time to run home and change.

This little afternoon break was about Cassie learning the truth, not a romantic getaway with Jesse. She'd been there and done that. Had the kid to prove it.

And wasn't interested in getting burned again.

No matter how much she was still attracted to him.

She knew he wasn't married, but that didn't mean he wasn't involved with someone. Taking a deep breath, she headed outside to find Cassie already waiting beside Jesse. He was driving a green van that looked as if it had seen many miles. She was glad they wouldn't be crammed into Jazz's truck or her small car.

"Hi." She hoped her nervousness wasn't obvious. "I'm free for the next two hours, barring an emergency."

"Let's go," Jesse said, gesturing toward the van. "I know of a great place where we can sit and watch the water."

She frowned when she noticed he was walking with a limp. "Something wrong?"

He darted a gaze at Cassie, then shook his head. "I'm fine."

Understanding he didn't want to discuss his latest injury

in front of their daughter, she let it go. She slid into the front passenger seat, while Cass crawled into the back.

"Whose booster seat?" Cassie asked.

"My nephew, Trey." Jesse carefully backed out of his parking spot. "This van belongs to my sister, Jemma. Trey is her son."

Carla knew about the McNally twins and their B&B. Personal issues aside, she was very glad they were bringing more tourists to the area. The grocery store needed all the help it could get.

The drive to Jesse's special spot didn't take long, although finding a parking space for the large van wasn't easy. Fifteen minutes later, they were walking down to a large flat rock overlooking the lake.

"This is cool!" Cassie climbed up on top of the rock without fear to peer over the edge. "I should have brought my swimming suit. I bet it would be fun to jump in from here."

"You shouldn't jump into the water without knowing how deep it is," Jesse warned, his eyes full of concern. "It's dangerous."

"The lake is super deep, isn't it, Mom?" Cassie looked to her for confirmation.

"In the middle, yes, but not necessarily close to the shore. Jesse is right, you shouldn't jump into water when you don't know how deep it is." She sat with her legs crossed on the flat surface, trying to think of a way to begin. "Listen, Cassie, there's something important I need to tell you."

"Is the store going under?" Cassie dropped beside her, giving her a hug. "It's okay, Mom. You'll find another job."

She glanced at Jesse and quickly shook her head. "No, honey, the store is fine. This is about you." The words seemed to stick in her throat. "About your father."

Now Cassie's face scrunched into a perplexed frown. "You told me my dad died before I was born."

Now it was Jesse's turn to frown, and she silenced him with a narrow glare. "I know that's what I told you, but the truth is that Jesse is your father."

Cassie's eyes grew wide, and she looked at Jesse with shocked surprise. "You are?"

Jesse nodded, his gaze uncertain. "Yes, I'm your father."

"You lied to me?" Cassie's hurt expression made her wince.

"I'm sorry, Cassie. I shouldn't have lied." She tried to think of a reasonable explanation, but there wasn't one.

Which only reinforced how wrong she'd been.

"Cassie, listen, I want you to know that it's my fault that I didn't know about you until now," Jesse said. "I left your mom to go off to college, and I didn't call her the way I promised."

"But—I don't understand." Cassie's expression mirrored her confusion. "You told me babies were made with love."

"Yes, that's true." Her cheeks burned with embarrassment, and she didn't dare look at Jesse. "But sometimes love doesn't last; adults grow up and go their separate ways. You have friends at school with parents who are divorced, right?"

Cassie nodded, and Carla felt a measure of relief. Having the birds and the bees talk wasn't something she wanted to have in front of Jesse.

"I'm sorry I didn't tell you the truth," she continued, reaching out to touch Cassie's shoulder. "That was wrong of me. And I really hope you can forgive me, Cass. Especially since Jesse didn't know about you until yesterday."

Jesse's eyes were suspiciously bright as he looked at their daughter. "I'm very glad to meet you, Cassie. I'm thrilled to be your dad. And I want you to know I'm planning to move to McNally Bay so I can see you more often."

Wait, what? He was? Carla was stunned speechless at the news. When had Jesse decided that? And what did it mean for her future? On one hand, she knew Cassie deserved to spend time with her father, but being close to Jesse, seeing him on a regular basis wasn't something she'd planned for.

Being with him now was bittersweet. He'd been her first and only love. When she'd gone to see him, only to find him kissing a beautiful blonde, her heart had been crushed beyond repair.

She'd gotten over him—out of sight, out of mind. Focusing on caring for Cassie and her mother after her father's death had helped. But if Jesse lived in McNally Bay, he'd be a constant reminder of how naïve and foolish she'd been.

"But if Mr. Jesse is my dad," Cassie said, "then how come my last name isn't McNally?"

"I, uh, well, your mom and I didn't get married," Jesse stuttered, the tips of his ears turning red. Carla was secretly glad he was just as uncomfortable with this as she was. "But I want you to know that I'm willing to adopt you as my daughter so you can share my last name."

Carla ground her teeth together in frustration. Maybe it was petty, but she wanted Cassie to share her last name, not take on Jesse's. "I'm not sure that's necessary," she quickly interjected. "Let's just see how things go, okay?"

"I guess that means I can't live in the McNally Mansion," Cassie said on a sigh.

"I don't live there either," Jesse said. "I'm only staying as a guest. It's a bed and breakfast now, remember?"

"Oh yeah, I forgot." Cassie fell silent for a moment, and

Carla waited for more questions about why she'd lied. But thankfully, her daughter seemed to have moved on. "Mom, does Grandma know Jesse is my dad?"

"No, but I'll tell her when I get home tonight." Carla knew that would be a far more difficult conversation than this one turned out to be.

"How about we get some ice cream?" Jesse seemed to sense her desire to move on.

"Okay! Mint chocolate chip is my favorite," Cassie said, jumping to her feet.

"Mine, too," Jesse confided. He stood, then offered his hand to help her up. "Do you still love raspberry?"

"Yes." It was ridiculous to feel happy that he'd remembered. His hand was warm around hers, and she found herself reluctant to let go.

Jesse drove them back into town and once again had to circle around to find a parking spot. Cassie chatted about how much she couldn't wait to tell her friends at school that she had a father after all, which only added to Carla's guilt. But she was ridiculously grateful the little girl wasn't holding a grudge.

"How is your mother going to take it?" Jesse asked in a low voice out of Cassie's earshot.

"Not sure." This wasn't the time to go into how her father had slapped her, then suffered a heart attack upon hearing the news.

"She's going to hate me, isn't she?" Jesse sounded dejected.

Before she could answer, Cassie was calling out with excitement. "Hey, look! It's Grandma!"

Carla frowned, her gaze following Cassie's. Sure enough, her mother was sitting on a bench in front of the Quilt

Shoppe beside Leon Tate. They were very close to each other, looking as if they spent a lot of time chatting.

"Grandma, guess what?" Cassie ran over to the older couple. "My daddy is Jesse McNally!"

Her mother's face paled, her gaze pinning Carla's with a sharp look of betrayal.

6

The daggers being aimed at him from Carla's mother spoke volumes. It was clear that a friend of Leon Tate's was no friend of the McNallys.

Carla stiffened beside him, and he knew that her life had irrevocably changed for the second time in the past nine years.

And both were his fault.

"I'm sorry," he said, putting a hand on her arm. "I guess your mom hates me as much as Leon Tate does."

"Yeah. And all this time, I thought it was only my father who hated your family." Carla's expression was pained as she watched her mother give Leon Tate a hug before standing up to take Cassie's hand in hers. "Guess I'll take a rain check on the ice cream."

"Don't." He gently held her arm to keep her from shrugging him off. "Let's not ruin this for Cassie. Look, it appears your mother loves Cassie more than she hates me."

"I wouldn't be too sure of that." Carla's voice held a note of desperation that made his heart ache for her. He would have done anything to make this situation better.

But he couldn't change who he was. Or who his father had been. And he didn't want to. Despite Carla's mother's feelings toward his family, he was proud of his grandparents and what they'd accomplished. He and his siblings were good people and didn't deserve to be hated with such intensity.

Helplessly, they stood and waited for Cassie and Carla's mother to approach. Irene Templeton looked pale and drawn as if she'd aged ten years in the past five minutes.

"Carla? Is it true?" Irene sent him a vengeful look as if everything that had gone wrong in the world was his fault. He wanted to think Carla's mother would be upset at any man who'd irresponsibly gotten her daughter pregnant, but he didn't believe it.

"Yes, Mom." Carla gave the woman a pleading look. "How about we discuss this more later, tonight, okay?"

In other words, not in front of Cassie.

The two women stared at each other for a full minute before Irene relented. Without saying a word to Jesse, the older woman turned to Cassie.

"I'll see you later, dear. I know you have to walk Bucky, but don't forget, dinner is at six."

"Okay, Grandma." Thankfully, his daughter didn't seem to notice the level of tension between the adults.

Without another word, Irene turned and walked away. Carla held herself stiffly, and he longed to draw her close for a reassuring hug.

"We're still having ice cream, right, Mom?" Cassie's tone was hesitant as if finally understanding everything wasn't quite normal.

"Of course." Carla's smile didn't reach her eyes. "Raspberry for me and mint chocolate chip for you and—" She stopped abruptly as if unsure how to refer to him.

"Listen, you both wait here, and I'll get our cones." He reluctantly let Carla go and headed over. The ice cream and hot dog stand wasn't far. It was a portable set up, only available on Main Street during the summer months. He paid for three cones, then carried them over to where Carla and Cassie waited.

Their outing wasn't turning out quite the way he'd hoped. Cassie's excitement at having him as a father was wonderful and more than he could have asked for. Yet seeing Carla's mom with Leon Tate explained a lot. He wondered if Carla's dad had been good friends with Leon Tate back in the days when his father had dated Leon's younger sister, Lucy.

"Thanks, Dad." Cassie took one of the mint chocolate chip cones from his hand and began to lick the melting cream from the edge of the brown sugar cone.

Hearing her refer to him as Dad made him smile. But his joy faded when he caught the glitter of tears in Carla's eyes.

"Are you okay?"

"Yes. Of course." Carla quickly swiped at her eyes before taking her raspberry ice cream.

He didn't like seeing her upset. "Maybe I should come over tonight so we can provide a united front." He chose his words carefully, hoping Cassie wouldn't pick up on what he meant.

"Um, no." Carla grimaced and avoided his gaze. "I'm fairly certain that would only make things worse."

He wanted to point out that they couldn't be much worse when he caught sight of a man standing off to the side, watching them intently.

Well, mostly watching Carla.

Was it possibly the same guy who'd hit him while riding past on a motorcycle? He narrowed his gaze, trying to remember. But the motorcycle rider had been wearing a helmet, and honestly, the guy watching them didn't seem the type. He was older than he and Carla were, in his estimate roughly eight to ten years.

"Who's that?" He jutted his chin toward the guy.

Carla followed his gaze, then let out a low groan. "Can this day get any worse?" she muttered.

"Worse?" Her comment hurt, more than it should. "Why? What's his problem?"

"Look, Mom, it's Principal Thomas." Cassie was gobbling up her ice cream faster than the adults were. "I told you he wants to ask you out on a date."

A date? Jesse frowned as a shaft of jealousy shot deep.

"Cassie, you need to stop saying that." Carla's tone was sharp. "I told you before we are just friends, nothing more. Now zip it."

"Okay, okay." Cassie's expression was chagrined. "Sorry."

Jesse filed that tidbit of information away for a future discussion. He told himself that he wasn't Carla's boyfriend anymore. That it shouldn't matter to him one way or the other whom she spent time with.

Yet thinking about Carla seeing another man made him want to punch something. It was ridiculous, they were both single adults with the right to date whomever they wanted.

But he didn't like it. Not one bit.

It hit him then how much his impulsive decision to move to McNally Bay was related to rekindling a personal relationship with Carla as much as being close to Cassie.

Unfortunately, he didn't get the impression Carla felt the same way about him. Especially given her mother's reaction to the news of his being Cassie's father.

He supposed he couldn't blame her. He'd been a jerk,

moving on with his life and not calling the way he'd promised. Although, she hadn't called him either.

But Carla had driven up to see him. Only to find him kissing another girl.

Enough. There was nothing they could do to change the past. He decided that from here on it was more important to focus on the future.

A future that included spending time getting to know his daughter.

CARLA FORCED herself to finish the ice cream, despite the growing pit of despair in her stomach. When they were finished, she ditched Jesse as soon as possible, making sure Cassie headed home to be with her grandmother before returning to the grocery store.

She dreaded the inevitable confrontation with her mother over Jesse being Cassie's father. Her mother had been so supportive nine years ago, never passing judgment upon having an eighteen-year-old daughter drop out of college because she was pregnant and alone.

But her mother's scathing glare only proved that her nonjudgmental attitude was a thing of the past. Apparently, Jesse being Cassie's father was unforgivable.

As she worked on the minute details that she needed to attend to, she found herself wondering if her mother would finally reveal the truth about why her father hated the McNallys so much. Was it too much to ask why the animosity existed between the two families for so many decades?

Although, did it really matter? No matter what had

happened in the past, it didn't change that Jesse planned to be involved in their daughter's life.

She hoped Jesse would be a good father to Cassie. Not distant and remote like hers. The way he'd grown teary while telling Cassie the truth had been humbling. He intended to be there for Cassie, and frankly, he was well within his rights to do so.

Her mother would just have to find a way to deal with it.

Brave words, but the impending sense of doom got worse as the day wore on. Even the fact that her second order of sparklers arrived on the four o'clock truck couldn't brighten her mood.

After locking up the store, she turned and headed home. Doing her best to brace herself for the worst, she opened the door of her mother's house and walked in.

"Hi, Mom!" Cassie tossed aside her book and rushed over to greet her with a hug. "Do you think it's okay if I spend the day with Dad tomorrow? He wants to take me out for a boat ride."

"You—uh—spoke to him?" She glanced over Cassie's shoulder to her mother.

"He came by with pizza from Gino's for dinner. He said he wanted to talk with Grandma." Cassie grinned. "He brought pepperoni, my favorite."

"He did?" Carla felt a bit as if she'd landed in another dimension. For some reason, it irked her that Jesse had bulldozed his way in without giving her a chance to talk things over with her mother.

Then again, it was in Jesse's nature to try to fix things. The same way he now fixed computer software issues.

"Grandma said she didn't like pepperoni pizza, but there's leftovers for you, Mom."

Oh boy. She could practically see the waves of anger rolling off her mother.

"Cassandra, it's time for you to get ready for bed." Her mother's tone was icy. "Go put on your jammies and brush your teeth."

"But, Grandma, it's not even dark outside yet."

"Listen to Grandma, I'll be in soon to tuck you in." She gave her daughter a nudge.

"Fine." Cassie stomped off toward her room.

"How could you?" her mother asked in a low voice the moment Cassie was out of the room. "Of all the boys in the area to give your virginity to, you had to pick Jesse McNally?"

"Stop it." Carla couldn't believe her mother was saying these things to her. "I loved Jesse. I . . . we didn't mean for it to happen."

"That's because you weren't thinking at all." Her mother's tone dripped with sarcasm.

"I'm not going to listen to you call me names." Carla tried to hide the way her hands were trembling. This was worse, so much worse than she'd anticipated. "Cassie is a blessing, not a mistake, and I won't allow you to treat me like dirt because I fell in love."

"Love." Her mother's tone was laced with bitterness. "You don't know the first thing about it. Where has he been all this time? Why is he just showing up now to take responsibility for what he's done? He should have been paying child support for the past eight years."

"That's enough." Carla lifted her chin and looked her mother directly in the eye. "If you must know, I didn't tell Jesse about Carla. He figured it out for himself. And so, by the way, did Betty Cromwell. You'd better brace yourself. The entire town will know the truth by morning."

The red flush of anger in her mother's face drained away as the realization sunk deep.

"You need to find a way to get over your hatred of Jesse McNally because he intends to relocate to McNally Bay. He wants to live here so he can be a part of Cassie's life."

"That can't be." Her mother swayed in a way that caused a flash of concern.

"Sit down, Mom." She hurried over to take her mother's arm, but she shrugged it away, stumbling over to the closest chair under her own power.

Carla curled her fingers into helpless fists. She loved her mother and couldn't stand the thought of something happening to her.

Being the cause of her father's death was bad enough.

She dropped to her knees beside her mother's chair. "Why, Mom? Why did you and Dad hate them so much?"

Her mother shook her head, then buried her face in her hands.

"Mom? Are you coming?" Cassie called.

She hesitated, waiting for her mother's response, but there was nothing forthcoming. Feeling as if she'd been battered by a tornado, she rose to her feet and went down the hall toward Cassie's room.

"Were you and Grandma fighting?" Cassie asked, her expression troubled.

"We're fine, nothing for you to worry about." She sat on the edge of Cassie's bed, smoothing a lock of hair from her face. Her daughter was a mini-me, looking so much like Carla had as a young girl. But after watching Cassie and Jesse together, she knew her daughter displayed many of the same McNally mannerisms.

It was surprising the lineage hadn't been discovered

before now. Still, she hated knowing how much she'd upset her mother.

"Can I spend the day with Dad tomorrow?" Cassie persisted. "Please?"

Tight bands of emotion cinched around her chest, a mixture of anger and resentment that Jesse had brought the subject up with Cassie without running it past her first. But despite her annoyance, she knew she couldn't deny her daughter's request to spend time with her father.

"Sure. But you can't forget your promise to take care of Bucky. Miss Daisy is counting on you."

Cassie's brow furrowed, then cleared. "I'll ask Miss Daisy if she'll let me take Bucky with us. He'll like that better than being in his crate."

Trust her daughter to come up with a reasonable solution. She nodded her agreement, then bent down to kiss Cassie's forehead. "Good night, Cass."

"Night, Mom." Cassie yawned, her eyes drooping as the excitement of the day finally caught up with her.

After leaving Cassie's room, she returned to the kitchen to talk to her mother, but she wasn't there. The door to her mom's room was closed, and Carla knew that as far as her mother was concerned the conversation about Jesse McNally was over.

It didn't make any sense that her mother had carried such a deep-seated grudge all these years. Made worse by the fact that her mother wouldn't provide an explanation.

Feeling restless, she went into her room. Sleep would be impossible, yet she still had an early day tomorrow. Resentment bubbled up in the back of her throat at the idea of Jesse and Cass spending the day together. Logically, she knew it was only fair, but she didn't like the thought of them being together without her.

A light tapping on her window had her jumping around in surprise, her heart thudding loudly in her chest. When she saw Jesse's face through the glass, she blew out her breath in a loud sigh. She crossed over and lifted the sash.

"What are you doing out there?" she asked in a loud whisper. "We're not eighteen anymore."

A wide grin split his features. "You remember."

She rolled her eyes in exasperation. "Of course, I remember. This is how we got ourselves in trouble. I should have sent you away."

His smile faded. "I know. You should have. But if you had, we wouldn't have Cassie."

That much was true. She sighed. "What do you want?"

"Come outside and talk to me." Jesse's engaging grin reminded her of how impossible it had once been for her to resist him.

But that was a long time ago.

"I have to be up early. Besides, I'm mad at you."

"I thought if I brought dinner your mother would maybe see that I'm not that bad," he protested. "But it didn't work."

"Not that." Although, she could have told him he was wasting his time. Her mother hadn't forgiven her, much less a McNally.

"Then what?"

"You had no right to invite Cassie out for a boat ride without talking to me first."

"I see." He nodded thoughtfully. "I'm sorry. This being a dad is new to me."

"Yeah, well, sharing Cassie with her father is new to me, too."

"I get it." He shrugged. "It didn't occur to me that you'd be upset. Carla, will you please come outside for a bit?"

She shouldn't, but she thought it wouldn't hurt to set some ground rules. "Okay, give me a minute."

"What, you're not going to crawl through the window like old times?" The hopeful expression on his face made her want to laugh, but she managed not to.

"No." She shut the window without saying anything more and then walked through the silent house to meet him outside.

Jesse was leaning against the wall outside her room, waiting for her. He straightened when she approached, and the way he looked in the dim light brought an avalanche of memories.

"Thanks for agreeing to talk," he said, his voice low and husky.

She nodded and crossed her arms over her chest as they walked away from the house. "I need you to check with me before making plans with Cassie, okay? And that includes dropping by with pizza."

"Yeah, well, your mother made that perfectly clear." He hesitated, then asked, "Did she you give you a hard time?"

"Yes." The argument came flooding back, and she was hurt by her mother's attitude all over again. "Nine years ago, she was sweet and supportive. Tonight, she was a different woman."

"It's because of me." Jesse took a step closer, reaching up to tuck a strand of her hair behind her ear. "I'm sorry she hates me. If there was something I could do to change it, I would."

"I know." She tried to smile but felt tears sting her eyes. Nine years ago, her mother had been her staunch supporter. And now the woman who'd loved her wouldn't look her in the eye.

"Shh, don't cry." Jesse pulled her into his arms, tucking

her head beneath his chin. "We'll get through this. I'll kill her with kindness. She can't hold out forever."

She let out a choked laugh at his never-ending optimism. His familiar scent filled her senses, making her realize how much she'd missed this.

Missed him.

"Don't hold your breath," she said, her voice muffled against his soft T-shirt.

"I won't. But I don't intend to give up either." He stroked his hand down her back, causing every nerve ending in her body to come alive.

The embrace changed from one of comfort to one of keen awareness. She told herself to step away, to put distance between them, but her feet refused to move.

"Carla." His low voice sent tingles down her spine. He placed a finger beneath her chin, then lowered his mouth to hers.

His kiss was everything she remembered, and more. So much more.

This was why she hadn't found a man. Why the very idea of going out on a date with Dean Thomas had filled her with abhorrence.

Jesse McNally was the only man who'd ever made her feel like this.

And he was the one man she could never have.

7

———

He hadn't planned on kissing her, but the moment their lips joined, he felt the familiar desire return full force.

Holding Carla close to his chest, their hearts beating in a simultaneous rhythm felt right. He wondered how he'd forgotten the special bond they'd shared. How he'd allowed himself to get sucked into the party scene at school when he should have been keeping his promise to Carla.

When she abruptly broke away from his embrace, he reluctantly let her go. "I'm sorry, I, uh, didn't mean for that to happen."

"I know." Carla wouldn't meet his gaze, and he wished he could see her more clearly in the dim light. The sun was still low on the horizon, but they were behind the house, her face cast in a shadow.

There was so much more he wanted, needed to stay, but for the life of him, he couldn't seem to think clearly. Carla's scent still had the ability to mess with his brain.

"I have to go." She'd crossed her arms over her chest in

the familiar defensive posture he'd noticed each time they saw each other. "I need to open the store by eight."

A flicker of annoyance caught him off guard. "It's a good excuse, but you can't hide behind your responsibilities at the store forever."

That had her jerking her head up to stare at him. "I'm not hiding behind anything. The store is my livelihood. I can't afford to be distracted by your desire to have a little fun."

It wasn't easy to hold back his temper, but he managed. "I'm going to send monthly child support payments, which should help."

"No! That's not what I meant." She raked her fingers through her hair. "Summer is the busiest time of the year for us. During the winter, I open later on the weekends and close earlier."

That answered one of his questions. He'd assumed the long winter months would be the most challenging. "Carla, Cassie is my responsibility, too. It's not fair for you to carry the financial burden of raising a child on your own. I would have been there for you if I'd known."

"So you said." Her tone didn't exude confidence. "Fine, go ahead and send child support payments. I'll put the money into her college fund."

Now she was pissing him off. "I can pay for her college, too. Just use the money, okay? For yourself or for Cassie, I don't care."

She hesitated, then finally nodded, and thankfully didn't pursue the argument further. He wondered if every discussion they'd have about Cassie would be like this. A battle of wills, before one of them caved in.

There was a long silence before she finally spoke. "What time are you and Cassie heading out tomorrow?"

"Probably around ten in the morning. I planned to pack food for lunch." He hesitated, then added, "I'd love for you to join us."

"I have to work." Her immediate response annoyed him.

"Yeah, I know. But you managed to leave for a few hours yesterday without the world coming to an end." He tried to cut back the sarcasm, but it wasn't easy. "What if I changed the time to eleven and we went out for a few hours together over lunch? I know you usually eat at the diner, but I'm sure Daisy won't mind packing a meal for us to go."

Her mouth thinned, but he could tell by the wistful expression in her eyes that she was giving serious consideration to his offer. Jesse found himself holding his breath while waiting for a response.

"I can do that," she finally said in a voice so soft he wondered if he'd imagined it. "Take a few hours off during lunchtime. But I need to be back by three thirty because we normally receive truck shipments of groceries around four in the afternoon."

It wasn't much, just over four hours, but he'd take it. "That would be great. I'm sure Cassie will be thrilled to have you along for the boat ride."

She nodded but didn't smile. He wondered if she was thinking about the argument she'd had with her mother. He felt bad about being the cause of friction between them, but not enough to give up the chance to be a part of his daughter's life.

Or Carla's.

"I'll pick up Cassie first, then swing by the grocery store after we get the food. The boat launch isn't far; we can probably walk from there."

"That works. Thanks for including me."

"Carla." He reached out to lightly touch her arm. "I

didn't intend to leave you out of our plans. You've made it clear the store keeps you busy, and I didn't want to upset you."

"It does keep me busy." She stared down at his hand on her arm for a long moment before stepping away, out of his reach. "But you're right about the fact that I can probably take a few hours off here and there. The store won't fall apart in the space of a few hours."

For a moment, he wished they could go back to that fateful summer, when they'd both been young and in love. Feeling carefree and full of anticipation for the future ahead. They'd shared their deepest hopes and dreams. He'd loved her so much.

He'd reached his dream of owning his own security software company, which had an excellent reputation for getting the job done. Avery and Arch aside, he was good at what he did. Maybe his personal life hadn't gone nearly as well, but he couldn't complain about his professional life.

But what about Carla's dreams? Obviously, she hadn't graduated from Iowa with her teaching degree. Running a grocery store in a small tourist town couldn't be that exciting. It wasn't what she'd wanted when they were young.

It wasn't right that he'd graduated with honors while she'd been stuck returning to the small town she couldn't wait to leave to have his baby.

"I really have to go," she said again. "I'll see you tomorrow around eleven."

"I'll be there." He tried to think of something more to say, some way of convincing her to stay with him for a while longer, but when she turned to walk back inside, he didn't try to stop her.

He waited until she'd gone inside before walking back toward Main Street, limping a bit from the brush with the motorcyclist. He'd reported the attack to Deputy Waldorf who had promised to investigate the incident.

Returning to the spot where he'd left Jemma's van, he kept a keen eye on his surroundings, hoping to catch another glimpse of the motorcycle. As a guy who knew and loved cars, he'd been able to tell Deputy Waldorf that the motorcycle had been a black Yamaha, the timbre of the engine was a distinct high-pitched humming sound, and the style was the kind where the rider hugged the bike as he or she drove. Distinct in some ways, but without a license plate number, impossible to pinpoint for certain.

But if he saw it again, he wouldn't hesitate to follow it in order to get a glimpse of the driver. The punch to his shoulder had been more annoying than painful, but his knee had hit the concrete hard, causing it to swell.

It was all so crazy. These personal attacks had to stop. He'd tried to find a motel to move to for the rest of his stay in McNally Bay, but with the Fourth of July holiday landing on Thursday, he'd discovered that everything close by was booked through the weekend.

He was glad the attacks were aimed at him personally, but he still didn't like the idea of bringing danger to the B&B.

Or worse, to Carla and Cassie. He needed to figure out what was going on, and soon. Before anyone close to him was hurt in the cross fire.

CARLA WENT to the store earlier than usual, partially to avoid another confrontation with her mother and partially to make sure she had everything taken care of inventory-wise so she could leave for a few hours.

Deep down, she was looking forward to spending some time with Jesse and Cass out on Lake Michigan. Living here in town, being near the water was great, but she didn't often have time to enjoy it.

Especially not since she'd taken over full responsibility of managing the store. Her mother had done her share for years, and it was now Carla's turn.

She hoped her mother would come around, at least to the point of being civil to Jesse. Holding on to a grudge and being angry wasn't healthy, physically or emotionally.

Her father was proof of how quickly extreme stress could bring on a heart attack. Although, she could see now that running the store could be stressful, too.

Shying away from the painful and guilt-ridden memories, she focused on the various tasks requiring her attention. Her small cramped office was located in the back of the store, not far from the general employee break room. And the supply storage area. She kept the door open, although she generally preferred peace and quiet while pouring over spreadsheets.

Thankfully, her young cashier showed up, not looking the least bit ill, which was one less thing to worry about. But as Carla worked, the idea of trying once again to find and hire an assistant manager wouldn't leave her alone.

It wouldn't hurt to advertise for one, maybe on one of those job seeker websites. She made a mental note to do that later in the afternoon, after the boat ride with Jesse.

His insistence on paying child support shouldn't bother her, but for some reason it did. Logically she knew that he should support Cassie; it was the right thing to do. But emotionally she didn't want to give him another reason to be included in decision-making surrounding her daughter.

Their daughter.

She sighed knowing that things would never be the same. She didn't begrudge Cassie the chance to know and love her father. Especially if Jesse was a better role model than her own dad. They both deserved to spend time together. But remembering their heated kiss was troubling. She thought she'd gotten over him.

But she hadn't. Not deep down, where it counted.

Her problem, not his. There was no reason he needed to know that her feelings for him hadn't ever gone away. Especially since she knew from firsthand experience the same couldn't be said for him.

Witnessing the way he'd kissed the blonde that night in Madison so many years ago had shaken the foundation of her being. It had proved that he'd never really loved her, the way he'd claimed.

And not the way she'd loved him.

Her parents had been right about Jesse being a player, and seeing him with the blonde had only confirmed their thoughts.

Whatever. Her feelings and his weren't the issue here. The important thing was to think about what was best for Cassie.

She vowed to do everything possible for her daughter.

"Ms. Templeton?"

She straightened in her seat, lifting her gaze to meet Sheryl's. "What is it?"

"A questionable return at the customer service desk. The sales slip has the Polish sausage being purchased two days ago, but it's well past expired."

"I'll take care of it, thanks." Carla rose to her feet and followed her senior cashier over to the counter. She wanted to groan when she noticed the person standing at the counter was Mary Tate.

Carla was fanatical about making sure she didn't sell expired food and knew very well that Leon and Mary Tate were always trying to get something for nothing. But they were friends of her mother, so she pasted a smile on her face and rang up the return.

"Here you go." She handed over the seven dollars and change.

"Thank you." Mary Tate sniffed. "You should watch your expiration dates closer. We could have died eating that sausage."

"I will." She kept the pasted smile on her face until Mary left, then quickly used the computer to pull up the Tate account. Offering a discount card where patrons earned points and extra coupons also provided a way to track their purchases.

She found the recent purchase of Polish sausage, then went back two weeks to find a previous purchase of the same item. They'd either forgotten about it or simply decided they didn't want to eat two packages of Polish sausage and found a way to get one returned so they could eat one for free.

Logging off the computer, she shook her head at the lengths some people would go for seven dollars. Deciding the Tates must need the money more than she did, Carla let it go.

Jesse arrived right on time, with Cassie, Bucky, and a large cooler full of food. It didn't take long for the three of them to walk down to the boat rental facility.

"You really know how to drive this thing?" She took a seat next to Cassie, who was holding on to Bucky, while he stuffed the cooler in the bow.

"It's got an engine, right?" He flashed a grin over his

shoulder as he started the engine. "I can drive just about anything."

She didn't doubt it but hung on tight as Jesse navigated out of the bay and into the deeper water of Lake Michigan. The breeze off the water felt wonderfully cool against skin warmed by the sun. There were dozens of watercrafts out on the lake, of various shapes and sizes, but Lake Michigan was big enough that it didn't feel overly crowded.

"Faster! Go faster!" Cassie urged, a broad smile on her face. Her daughter was dressed in jean shorts and a tank top with a life jacket pulled over the clothes, her hair pulled back in a ponytail. In that moment, Cassie was reminded of herself at the same age. Her father worked long hours at the store, and those rare days he wasn't working, he'd made degrading comments about her shorts and tank tops. It seemed that she could never please him, but as it turned out, maybe he had a right to be worried since she had ended up pregnant. She'd been hurt by her father's attitude and secretly glad her mother had always stuck up for her.

Carla wanted to maintain a good relationship with her daughter, too, unwilling to let her responsibilities at the store impinge on their relationship.

Even Bucky looked around with interest, his tongue lolling out as he lifted his curly face to the wind.

"A girl after my own heart," Jesse yelled as he pushed the boat to go faster. The water was relatively calm for Lake Michigan, but the boat still went up and slapped down on the water with a regular motion that threatened to make her dizzy.

Cass reveled in the speed, proving she was indeed her father's daughter. Jesse headed pretty far away from shore but then eventually turned back around.

"That was awesome!" Cassie beamed with excitement. "Will you teach me to drive a boat?"

"When you're older," Jesse promised. Then he shot a guilty look at her over his shoulder and added, "If your mom says it's okay."

"When she's older," Carla agreed, grateful he'd remembered.

"Aw, Mom. That's what you always say. You won't even let me have my own phone."

"That's right. Not until you're thirteen." She pinned Jesse with a look that told him he better not argue with her on this.

He didn't, smart man. "Thirteen is reasonable."

Cassie let out a huff but then turned her attention back to the controls of the boat. Bucky was curled up beside her as if the ride had worn him out. "Show me how it works."

Jesse went over the basics while Cass listened with rapt attention. Carla was amazed at his level of patience and his ability to explain something complicated in a way their daughter could understand.

For lunch, Jesse headed over to a spot near the shoreline where he dropped anchor. Daisy outdid herself with the picnic. They had thick roast beef sandwiches, fresh fruit and coleslaw, and peach cobbler for dessert. She'd even packed a couple of cookie bones for Bucky, who scarfed them down in record time.

"I have to stop eating like this." With a groan, Carla put her empty dish of cobbler back inside the cooler. If she didn't watch out, she'd gain five pounds just by spending time with Jesse throughout the remainder of the week.

"It was so yummy," Cassie said with a grin. She rubbed Bucky's fur, then asked, "Can I go swimming?"

"Did you bring your bathing suit?" Jesse asked.

"No, but I can swim in my shorts."

Jesse grimaced and looked at her as if needing confirmation that it was a bad idea.

"Maybe next time, Cass. We don't have towels either, and lake water will be colder than you realize. When the wind hits you, you'll be freezing. Especially since he drives so fast."

"He does." Cassie's disappointment over not being allowed to swim didn't last long. "It would be fun to swim, and I want to go fishing next time, too."

They lounged in the sun for a little while longer before Jesse turned the boat back toward McNally Bay. As promised, he had her back at shore by three thirty in the afternoon.

She was disappointed their time together was over, but she knew she needed to get back to the store. Especially since their afternoon truck was due to come in. She needed to make sure they received everything she'd ordered.

"Thanks, Jesse, this was wonderful."

His smile lit up his entire face. "I thought so, too." He moored the boat, then held out his hand to her so she could step out of the boat and onto the pier.

His hand was warm and strong as he helped her off the craft. He did the same with Cassie who carried Bucky out, before grabbing the cooler.

"I'll walk you back to the store, before returning the cooler and Bucky back to Miss Daisy," Jesse said.

"There's no need to walk me back. I go this way every day on my own."

"We'll walk together, right, Cassie?"

"Right," her daughter agreed. She held Bucky's leash, keeping him close, and they all went together, looking very much like the happy little family Betty had called them, back to the grocery store.

As they approached the parking lot, her steps slowed when she caught a glimpse of Dean Thomas standing near the front door of the store, looking down at his watch as if waiting for something.

Waiting for her?

"Mom, isn't that Principal Thomas?"

"What?" Jesse came to an abrupt halt, his gaze narrowing with anger. "What is up with that guy anyway?"

Good question. The way Dean Thomas kept showing up wherever she happened to be felt distinctly stalker-ish. "I don't know. I made it clear I wasn't interested."

At that moment, Dean looked up and saw her standing there with Jesse on one side and Cassie on the other. There was a flash of anger in his eyes before he abruptly straightened and turned to head inside the store.

"You're not going in there alone," Jesse said. "We'll go with you."

"Bucky can't come inside," she protested. "Just take care of Cassie, okay? I'll be fine. There are plenty of people inside."

It was obvious Jesse didn't like it, but he reluctantly nodded his agreement. He and Cassie turned and headed down Main Street toward Daisy's Diner.

Steeling her resolve, Carla entered the store. If Dean kept this up, she'd have no choice but to call the police.

8

Jesse mulled over the fact that Dean Thomas, the principal of Cassie's elementary school, had been waiting for Carla outside the grocery store while making sure he walked Cassie and Bucky back to the diner. After seeing them safely inside, he returned to the B&B.

He had to wonder if the guy was behind the attacks against him and the damage to his car. While he wasn't a cop, being involved with computers gave him a logical way of thinking, and as he reviewed the timeline, he realized it didn't quite add up. He hadn't even known about Cassie being his daughter when he'd arrived at Daisy's on Monday. He'd found out a short while later and hadn't even left the diner before the damage had been done.

Unless—was it possible Thomas had seen him talking to Carla through the window? Nah, it seemed a stretch to think the principal had figured out which car belonged to him. Sure, a cherry red Corvette stood out among other cars, but it didn't carry a vanity plate with his name on it or anything.

While it may not be as likely that one of the locals drove an expensive Corvette, he was convinced that people vacationing from Detroit or Chicago did. And there were plenty of tourists crowding Main Street.

It didn't make any sense, but once he pulled into the parking area in front of the B&B, he decided to place a call to Deputy Waldorf to give her the latest update.

"Dean Thomas?" Doubt laced her tone. "He's the principal of the elementary school."

Which didn't make him a saint, but Jesse tried to hold back his annoyance. "I'm telling you, the guy is obsessed with Carla Templeton. I've seen him twice now watching her from afar. At the very least, you need to investigate whether or not he owns a motorcycle or was seen anywhere near Daisy's on Monday during the lunch hour."

"Hang on a moment." He could hear the clattering of the deputy's fingers on the keyboard. "He owns a Dodge Ram pickup truck and a fishing boat. No motorcycle."

"But he could rent one."

"Anyone can rent anything," Deputy Waldorf responded dryly. "Listen, Jesse, I'd need a warrant to get access to his credit cards, and I don't think your suspicions are enough to get one signed by a judge. Even here in a small town, we tend to follow the same rules as the big city guys do."

"Yeah, okay." He blew out a frustrated breath, wishing there was more he could do or say to convince her. There was something off about the guy. "Will you do me one last favor?"

"Maybe."

"Talk to Carla Templeton. Thomas may not be the one responsible for the attacks against me, but the way he's watching Carla is creepy. I think he needs to hear from law enforcement the definition of stalking as identified by state statute."

"Sure, I can do that." The deputy's voice sounded relieved, and he knew she was absolutely convinced Thomas wasn't involved in the attacks against him. He wished he could be so sure. "Jesse, how long will you be in town?"

"I'm supposed to head back to Chicago on Sunday, but I'm not sure if I'm doing that yet." His car was still being repaired, so if he did go back on Sunday, he'd have to fly. Still, he'd told both Carla and Cassie that he'd relocate to McNally Bay yet hadn't even started looking at potential places to live. His sisters would certainly offer the B&B, but he'd honestly prefer to be in town, closer to Carla and Cassie. As much as he didn't like it, he may have to return to Chicago for a while before he could make the move official.

"Watch your back," Deputy Waldorf said, interrupting his thoughts.

"I will." He disconnected from the line and stared for a moment out the windshield of Jemma's van. He'd promised his sisters that he'd have dinner with them tonight, but maybe after that he could start scoping out a place to live. Most of the vacant houses were rented during the summer, but something should open up by fall.

The heat of the sun pouring in through the windows made him push out of the van to head inside. When he entered the great room, he stopped short when he saw that the young couple were seated across with Jemma enjoying a late afternoon snack. His sister's blond hair was pulled back from her face, her brown eyes full of anticipation. He'd forgotten that Jemma had mentioned offering a tea of sorts to her guests each day.

"Hi, Jesse." Jemma jumped to her feet, treating him as a guest rather than a member of the family. "Come in and have a seat. What can I get you to drink? Iced coffee or tea? Or lemonade?

"Lemonade sounds great." He smiled at the young couple cuddled close on the sofa. "Good afternoon."

"Jesse, this is Rachel Martin and Eric Humphreys. They're looking at booking a wedding here next year." Jemma beamed, and he knew she was thrilled with the idea of booking weddings almost a year in advance. "I'll be right back with your lemonade. Help yourself to my oatmeal and raisin cookies."

He wasn't hungry, thanks to the impromptu picnic on the boat, but gladly accepted the lemonade. The young engaged couple raved about the photos that were taken during Jazz and Dalton's wedding, which were also posted on the website for marketing purposes, while discussing options for their own nuptials.

When the couple moved on, he rose to his feet to do the same. Only Jemma held up a hand to stop him.

"Hold it," she commanded. "What's this we're hearing of Cassie Templeton being your daughter?"

With an inward groan, he wanted to smack himself for not mentioning it sooner. He'd forgotten that news traveled fast through the grapevine, even reaching the outskirts of town where the McNallys' B&B was located.

"It's true," he admitted, looking his sister directly in the eye. "But understand, I only just found out on Monday. Carla didn't tell me prior to this, or things would have been very different. And we didn't get a chance to tell Cassie the news until yesterday. I know I should have filled you and Jazz in, too."

"Yes, it was quite the shock for Jazz to hear the news from Mrs. Cromwell while at the hardware store." Jemma came over to rest her hand on his arm. "Jesse, are you sure she's yours?"

"Absolutely. And if you watched Cass for any length of time, you'd see the family resemblance for yourself. She looks like her mom, but she has definite McNally mannerisms. In fact, that was how I knew she was mine. She smiled and reminded me of Jazz."

"Wow. That must have been a shock." Jemma's gaze was troubled, and he knew he wasn't getting away until he'd told her the rest.

After providing a quick overview, ending with how upset Carla's mother, Irene Templeton, was about a McNally being the father of Carla's child, he flashed a lopsided smile. "Obviously, I need to figure out a way to relocate here to McNally Bay. It won't be easy. I'll have to drive back and forth into Grand Rapids or Kalamazoo for access to an airport. But I intend to be a part of my daughter's life." And Carla's too, but he wasn't going to mention that just yet.

"You're welcome to stay here in the master suite," Jemma quickly offered. "This is as much your home as ours."

"Thanks, but give me some time to evaluate my options." He didn't want to point out that living in a B&B wasn't exactly what he was looking for. The constant ebb and flow of guests coming and going would drive him crazy. Besides, it was a car ride into town to see Carla and Cassie when he'd rather be close at hand.

"Even for the short term," Jemma persisted. "We'd love to have you."

"I appreciate it, Sis." He reached out to give her a one-armed hug. "Again, sorry you found out through the town gossip."

"We're used to Mrs. Cromwell," Jemma said with a wave of her hand. "The way she's been seeing Mayor Henry Banks, we're all figuring she'll be announcing her own wedding soon enough."

"True. Hey, maybe she'll book a gazebo wedding!" Jemma groaned. He smiled and glanced at his watch. He had just enough time to start combing the internet for properties in the area. "Do you know anyone in the realtor business?"

"Jazz and Dalton worked with a Melanie something-or-other when they purchased the old Stevenson place. I'm sure one of them still has her contact information."

"Great, thanks." He figured he'd talk to Dalton at dinner. "See you in a few."

He walked through the kitchen and dining area to the master suite. After pulling his laptop out of his bag, he booted it up. First, he'd see what might be for sale, then reach out to the realtor Jazz and Dalton had used.

The sooner he found a place to live in town, close to Carla and Cassie, the better. He didn't trust that Dean Thomas guy not to do something crazy.

CARLA BRACED herself for a confrontation with Dean, but as it turned out, he bought a few things, then left without saying a word to her.

She was relieved he hadn't created a scene. Maybe she'd misunderstood what he'd been doing outside the store. There was no reason to assume he'd been waiting for her.

Except, she'd caught the flash of irritation in his gaze when he'd noticed she was with Jesse.

Pushing the issue of Dean Thomas aside, she waded

through the myriad of problems needing her attention. Just like the day before, the store staff seemed to function fine without her, at least for a few hours.

As the hours passed, Carla braced herself for the inevitable confrontation with her mother. It hurt that the woman who'd been so wonderfully supportive was now angry and aloof. Refusing to discuss why she was so upset with learning Cassie's father was Jesse McNally.

Frankly, she'd always assumed her mother had guessed the truth long ago. The similarities between her daughter and Jesse McNally were so obvious. There were times Cass reminded her of Jazz, too. She supposed it was a blessing her daughter shared her own hair and eye color, or the truth would have been uncovered long ago.

The way it should have been, she silently acknowledged as she closed up the store and locked the door. Jesse was right. She could have called him to let him know she was coming.

Easy enough to blame the lack of foresight on the fact that she'd been dealing with shocking news, but deep down, she knew that wasn't completely accurate.

She'd wanted to surprise him. To see how he reacted to seeing her without knowing she carried their child. To see if he had any lingering feelings for her.

Witnessing how he'd kissed the blonde had convinced her Jesse didn't love her, and really, probably never had. At least, not the way she'd loved him. Hurting from the sting of rejection, she'd been overwhelmed even further by her father's reaction and subsequent heart attack.

It occurred to her that maybe that was the main reason her mother resented the McNallys. Could it be she blamed Carla for her father's death? That hadn't been the case at the time, her mother had assured her that her father had complained of chest pains earlier but refused to do anything about it.

Yet now, looking back, she wondered if her mother just couldn't handle it. That seeing Jesse McNally was a reminder of how her husband had clutched his chest and dropped to the ground upon hearing the news.

Pushing away the depressing thoughts, Carla left the store. She swept a gaze over the parking lot, confirming no cars lingered. And she couldn't help looking over her shoulder every few steps as she made her way home. There was no sign of Dean Thomas, or anyone else for that matter. By the time she reached the house she shared with her mother, she had convinced herself that she was overreacting to seeing Dean lounging outside the grocery store.

Even if he hadn't gotten the message when she'd told him she wasn't interested, he must realize it now.

Her mother and Cassie were seated at the kitchen table playing Gin Rummy when she entered the house. Without making eye contact, her mother gestured toward the fridge. "There's a plate of spaghetti in there for you."

"Thanks." She glanced at the cards they were playing as she pulled the meal out and proceeded to reheat it in the microwave. "Who's winning?"

"Me!" Cass sounded smug.

"Not for long," her mother warned. She picked up a card off the deck and let out a shout. "Gin!"

"Aw, Grandma. Are you kidding me?" Cassie looked disappointed and frowned when her mother displayed her hand. "Rats."

"Time to get ready for bed." Her mother gathered the cards into a pile.

"Okay." Cassie didn't argue but jumped up and came over to give her a quick hug. "Thanks for the fun day today. I hope we can rent a boat again really soon."

"You're welcome." She returned her daughter's hug, noticing the tightness in her mother's face as Cass mentioned the boat ride they'd taken with Jesse. "Now do as Grandma told you, brush your teeth, wash your face, and get into your pajamas."

"You know it's still light out, right?" Cassie said in an adultlike tone before disappearing down the hall toward her room.

Carla pulled the plate out of the microwave and carried it over to the table. She dropped into the seat across from her mother. "Mom, we need to talk."

Her mother concentrated on putting the cards in a neat pile as if they were the most important thing in the world. It was a long moment before she looked up. "There's nothing to discuss." Her tone was as cold as ice.

Carla fought the urge to roll her eyes. Her mother could be very stubborn when she wanted to be. It had been a constant battle over chemo and radiation appointments, too. Her mother wanted to do everything alone, even when she was puking her guts out. Her mother's determination to be strong had eventually faded when her body hadn't been able to keep up with her will.

The memory of those rough days had her softening her tone. "Do you want me to apologize, Mom? Because I will. I'm very sorry for putting you through this. I never intended to hurt you or Dad."

Her mother stared down at her hands for a long moment without speaking. Carla took a bite of spaghetti, even though the conversation was pretty much ruining her appetite.

"I was young and foolish and in love." Carla was almost whispering now, not wanting Cassie to overhear. "You raised me right, but I ignored your rules. If I could go back and do things differently . . ." Her voice trailed off because she couldn't say it. Couldn't say she wouldn't do it again.

Cassie was so much a part of her life she couldn't regret what had happened nine years ago. Oh sure, maybe the way it had transpired, without Jesse being there to provide support, or how the news had impacted her father's health.

But not the fact that she'd given birth to a beautiful, spunky, and smart little girl.

Her mother still hadn't said anything, which was worrisome. There had never been a rift like this in their relationship, and she didn't like that it was happening now.

"Mom, please don't take your anger toward me and Jesse out on Cassie. She is the true innocent in all of this. She needs you. I need you." Tears stung her eyes, and she tried to blink them away.

"I'll always love you and Cassie," her mother finally said, her voice thick with emotion. "But you'll have to forgive me if I can't say the same about Jesse McNally."

"Why?" She leaned forward, taking her mother's hand in hers. "Because he got me pregnant? You know I carry just as much blame for that. It was both of us who wanted to be together, not just Jesse."

"Mom, I'm ready for bed!" Cassie's voice broke into their intense conversation.

"Coming, Cass," Carla called without taking her eyes off her mother's. She didn't want the conversation to end like this. "I don't understand why you and Dad hated Jesse and his family so much. He hated them before he knew I was pregnant, right? Just tell me why."

Again, there was a long pause before her mother

answered. "For years, the McNally family acted as if they owned this town. It was the height of arrogance to name the bay after themselves, but that's exactly what they did. Or their ancestors did."

"Okay." Carla was trying to understand why the name of the town mattered so much.

"I grew up here, just as your father did." Now her mother looked her in the eye. "Your dad was good friends with Leon Tate, and his younger sister, Lucy, was my best friend."

A warning tingle raised the hair on the back of her neck. This explained why her mother had been sitting so close to Leon Tate yesterday.

"Lucy was in love with Justin McNally. She was sixteen. Justin was a year older. He took her out on a boat ride late at night, well past dusk, along with a few of his friends. Something happened, an altercation of sorts. No one ever said for sure, but it doesn't matter. The outcome was the same. Lucy died that night." Her mother's blunt statement struck deep. "And we all knew Lucy's death was Justin's fault. He was the one driving the boat."

The last part didn't make sense to Carla, but she didn't want to interrupt her mother's story.

"That wasn't even the worst part," her mother continued. She was staring off into the distance as if reliving those moments all those years ago.

"What was?" she felt compelled to ask.

Her mother's gaze swung to hers. "The worst part is that I know Justin did it on purpose. He made sure Lucy died that night because she'd told him she was pregnant."

Pregnant? Carla sucked in a harsh breath, stunned at the revelation. It explained so much. Her father's over-the-top reaction to news of her pregnancy and the lasting resentment toward the entire McNally family.

Right or wrong, her mom firmly believed Justin McNally murdered Lucy Tate to hide the fact that he'd gotten her pregnant.

9

———

Jesse awoke bright and early to the incessant buzzing of his phone. Squinting against the harsh sunlight, he blindly reached out to find the device. Blinking the fog from his eyes, he peered at the screen.

Brian.

With a groan, he let the call go to voice mail. He was tired of Brian's seemingly endless requests to get him to return to Chicago sooner than planned. It wasn't as if Jesse took vacations very often, surely he was allowed one lousy week off work.

But looking closer at the screen, he realized there were several missed calls from his partner, all from the past ninety minutes.

Something must be really wrong.

Great. Just great. Swinging upright, he dragged his hands over his face in an attempt to get rid of the remnants of sleep. It was barely seven o'clock in the morning. Normally, he was up early, but Brian was a night owl all the way.

Concern had him calling Brian back. "What's wrong? Is

the company going under?" It was the only reason he could think of that Brian would be calling nonstop so early.

"It will if you don't get back to Chicago. Our company computer system is infected with some sort of virus."

"What?" Jesse came awake with a sharp intensity. Rising to his feet, he began to pace. "What do you mean? What kind of virus? How is that even possible?"

"I'm not sure, but I can't access my files. Our proprietary software program is frozen. Can you try on your end?" Brian's voice held a note of panic.

"Yes. Give me a minute." Jesse put the call on speaker and then opened his laptop and logged in. His sisters had installed password-protected Wi-Fi at the B&B, so he was able to go into their Software Solutions, Inc site without difficulty.

Only he couldn't. He got as far as the main page, but the entire system was frozen exactly as Brian had told him.

A shiver snaked down his spine. This wasn't good.

"Something is very wrong," Jesse said, more to himself than to Brian.

"I know. I've been trying to go in to fix it but haven't had any luck. I really need you to come back, Jesse. This could destroy our entire business, not just because we can't use our own computer system, but just think of what might happen if word gets out that the infamous duo who saves other companies' computer software systems has been brought down by a virus. It could be the end of everything we've worked for."

"Yeah, okay." He couldn't deny this was a serious issue that needed to be resolved as soon as possible. "But it's going to take me a while. I don't have a car and will need to get a ride to the closest airport, which is pretty far away. Plus, my sisters are busy until after breakfast time, so I probably won't even be able to get out of here until mid to late morning."

He could ask Carla, but then he rejected that idea. She'd be busy running the store. It would be easier for Jazz or Dalton to give him a ride.

"I get it." Brian sounded relieved to know he would be returning soon. "And I'm sorry about this. I'll keep investigating the issue from my end. We must have suffered some sort of viral attack. Just do your best to get here, okay?"

"Yeah, okay." Jesse disconnected from the call, battling a wave of frustration. The company he and Brian had built from nothing was important. It was their livelihood. Yet the timing sucked. He wasn't ready to leave Carla and Cassie. Plus, he'd found a small house not far from town that happened to be for rent as of the first of September. It wasn't ideal to wait that long, but it was the closest property he'd found within walking distance of Main Street, and he planned to jump on it.

After a quick shower and shave, he headed out to the dining area for breakfast, bringing his laptop computer with him. He chose a table overlooking Lake Michigan, figuring it would be nice to enjoy the view for the little time he had left.

While he knew it was best to use the main computer in his home office, he figured it wouldn't hurt to get a jump start on investigating what was wrong by using his laptop.

Brian should be able to fix the problem, too. They'd been college roommates, and both had the same degree in computer science. It was how their business had been formed, by combining their strengths into a troubleshooting computer software restoration business. He squelched a flash of annoyance at Brian's request for his help. His partner had been preoccupied lately, and he knew they needed to talk.

But not now. First, he needed to get their software program up and running.

Thankfully, his personal laptop was loaded with powerful software. As Jazz brought him fresh coffee, a cranberry muffin, and a slice of lemon poppy-seed bread, he began running a diagnostic program, going in through the back door of their personal security system. The one he and Brian had created.

"You want the full Irish again?" Jazz asked. "Or do you want to try Jemma's infamous French toast?"

He glanced up at Jazz with a distracted smile. "Um, the French toast sounds good."

"Something wrong?" Jazz gestured with her free hand toward his computer.

"Yeah, you could say that. I'm going to need to fly home for a few days. Do you think you or Dalton can drive me to the airport once I find a flight?"

"Of course, but I thought you wanted to stay the week." Jazz's expression mirrored her disappointment. "Tonight is the Fourth of July. We were planning a large barbeque outside and wanted to invite Carla and Cassie to join us. You know, our way of welcoming them to the McNally family."

He was touched by Jazz and Jemma's efforts and wished once again he could have had just a few more days here in McNally Bay. "That's very nice of you, but we can still do that. Just postpone it for a few days. Once I get this issue resolved, I'll come back, okay?"

"Sure, I understand." Jazz managed a sad smile before returning to the kitchen, leaving him to focus on the diagnostic program he was running on his laptop.

"Oh yeah, there you are," he muttered as the program

picked up a Trojan horse virus. "I've got you, but how in the world did you get in there anyway?"

Talking to himself was a bad habit he'd picked up through hours of working alone on computer systems. He managed to isolate the virus, then sat back in his chair, sipping his coffee as he considered the best way to dismantle the hold it had on their operating system. He texted Brian to back off working on the problem, not wanting to create more issues by having both of them poking around in the security system.

He was still thinking when Jazz brought him a plate of Jemma's infamous French toast. He pushed the laptop aside, remembering all the great reviews he'd seen online related to Jemma's cooking.

"Thanks, Jazz. And thank Jemma, too." After adding a dollop of maple syrup, homemade from a farm located in Clark County, he dug in.

Man, oh man. It was just as good as the reviewers had claimed. As he devoured every morsel, he continued dissecting the virus problem in the back of his mind.

Knowing he should look for the next available flight out of either Kalamazoo or Grand Rapids, he instead dawdled over his coffee. It occurred to him that if he could find a way to fix the virus from here via his laptop, he wouldn't have to travel back to Chicago today.

Fueled with enthusiasm at the possibility of being able to stay in McNally Bay to finish out his week, he pushed his empty plate aside and went to work.

It wasn't easy. Jesse took a break after an hour. He needed to walk away, to regroup. His hopes of sticking around were fading fast. He decided to check on available flights out of Kalamazoo, as it was closest. There was a flight to Chicago leaving at five o'clock in the afternoon.

Glancing at his watch, he grimaced. It was already nine thirty in the morning. Kalamazoo was roughly one hundred and twenty miles from McNally Bay, and the airport was even a bit further out, servicing both Kalamazoo and Battle Creek. He needed to get to the airport by three o'clock at the latest, and it would easily take them close two and a half hours to get there.

That gave him a little more than three hours to break through the Trojan horse virus and to repair the damage.

With reluctance, he purchased the one-way ticket, hoping, praying he wouldn't need it. Then took a quick moment to pack his stuff.

He intended to work all the way up to the noon hour if necessary. Jazz brought him more coffee. He thanked her, then requested the ride he'd likely need to get to the Kalamazoo airport.

"Sure thing. I'll be happy to take you." Jazz gestured to his table. "Looks like you're settling in, but I need to go up and clean some rooms. Jemma's working on cleaning up the kitchen, too, but I can ask her to keep the coffee going."

"That would be great. I may need it." He shooed her away. "Go on, do whatever you need. I'm going to see if I can't fix the issue before we need to hit the road."

"Okay. Although, you may want to talk to Carla and Cassie before you go."

He winced, belatedly realizing she was right. "Yeah, okay. Just give me some time to work first. If it's not looking good, we can leave a little earlier so I can stop by the grocery store on the way." It wasn't optimal, but it was the best he could do if he wanted to stay.

"If you say so." Jazz didn't seem too impressed with his plan.

Pushing those thoughts aside, he went back to work. He

needed to find a way to eliminate the virus without an impact to their operating system.

A task proving far easier said than done.

CARLA STEWED about the story of Lucy Tate's death as she worked. When she had to review the inventory twice, because she hadn't been paying attention, she pushed it away.

Today was the Fourth of July, but they always kept the store open over the holiday. There would be last-minute dashes to the store to pick up food for barbeques and snacks for parties. There was already a serious dent in her second shipment of sparklers, and she wished she'd purchased more because the markup was better than that on most of the food items.

It wasn't easy to make a living off a grocery store. Food went bad, especially produce, and it wasn't easy to figure out what people were interested in buying. She did her best to make sure old produce and meat nearing their expiration date didn't go bad by purchasing them herself, but still, the amount of food that was discarded each week was criminal.

She'd half expected Jesse to stop by, asking to meet her and Cassie for lunch. When he still hadn't shown up by eleven thirty, her annoyance grew. Did he think he could just show up whenever he wanted? To simply barge in on the alone time she normally spent with her daughter?

Even if at some point they agreed on some sort of co-custody arrangement, it wasn't as if he could just pop in and out without notice. These sorts of things had to be planned ahead of time.

As the hour inched closer to noon, she finished up the

last of the paperwork and headed outside. When she saw Jesse striding toward her, looking as handsome as ever with a broad grin on his face, her ire faded fast, and it was all she could do not to run and throw herself into his arms.

Instead, she tried to hold on to her previous annoyance. "What are you doing here?"

"Looking for you." Jesse reached for her hand, but she took a step backward to avoid him. He frowned, sensing she was upset. "I'm sorry I couldn't get here sooner, but I spent the morning reconstructing my company's operating system after being hacked by a virus. But I fixed it, just in the nick of time."

"You did?" She felt ashamed of her petty irritation. She had no idea he'd actually been working.

"Yeah, it was touch and go for a while there." He shook his head with a rueful smile. "I almost had to fly back to Chicago to take care of it, but I managed to fix the problem remotely. I gave myself a deadline of noon and managed to finish everything by eleven forty-five."

Fly back to Chicago? She struggled not to reveal how hard the news hit. "I, um, didn't you say something about relocating?"

"You bet. In fact, I have an appointment with a realtor named Melanie Ryerson at two this afternoon." His gaze held a note of uncertainty. "I was hoping you might be able to spare some time to go with me."

"Ah, sure. That would be great." She gestured toward Daisy's. "I'm meeting Cassie for our usual lunch date. You're welcome to join us if you're interested."

"I'd like that." He looked pleased at the offer, and she silently berated herself for giving in so quickly. What was wrong with her anyway? It was as if she couldn't be mad at Jesse no matter what he did.

"Oh, and I'm supposed to extend an invitation to you and Cassie to come to the McNallys' B and B for a big Fourth of July dinner tonight," he added, falling into step beside her.

"Dinner? At a B and B?" She headed toward the diner, sending Jesse a confused look. "That doesn't make sense."

"This is Jemma and Jazz's way of welcoming you and Cassie to the family."

Her thoughts veered for a moment to her mother and her deep dislike of the McNallys. Even though Carla knew it was ridiculous to extend the sins of the father to Jesse and his siblings, her mother would not be happy to hear about a *welcome to the family* party.

"I don't know if that's a good idea," she hedged as they approached the diner. "I don't want Cassie to think she's going to be moving into the mansion anytime soon."

"She won't, we already told her it's a B and B." Jesse put a hand to stop her. "Come on, Carla. Tell me what's really going on."

"You know what the problem is," she countered. "My mother isn't going to like knowing we're having dinner at the mansion. She doesn't like you, remember?"

"I know, I'm the jerk who got you pregnant." His expression turned somber. "I totally get that. But she loves Cassie, and I have to think she'll get over her hatred of me eventually."

"Listen, Jesse, she told me the real reason she and my father hated your family. It goes way back."

He lifted a brow. "I figured as much when I saw your mom all cozy with Leon Tate. I'm sure he's filled her with all sorts of heinous stories about my dad. But I'm telling you, they're not true."

"Are you so sure about that?" She glanced around,

looking for signs Cassie might be nearby. She didn't want her daughter to overhear what her mother had confided.

"Yes." He sounded confident. "I know that my dad dated Lucy and that he was driving the boat the night she fell overboard and drowned. And Leon Tate blames my dad because his younger sister wouldn't have even been on the boat that night if it wasn't for the fact that she and my dad were in love. But the truth is, my dad was heartbroken afterward. We found a letter in the attic addressed to Lucy from my dad."

"Letter?" Her heart thumped wildly in her chest, and she grabbed his arm. "You found a letter?"

"Yeah. Jemma was up in the attic looking for the old silver candlesticks my grandmother had stored up there and found it tucked into the family Bible."

"The family Bible?" She felt a bit like a parrot repeating everything he said. She pulled herself together. "I'd like to see the letter, if you don't mind."

"I don't mind." Jesse waved a hand as Cassie and Bucky approached. "But that means you and Cassie will have to join us for dinner." He raised his voice louder. "Hi, Cass, how are you?"

"I was hoping you'd be here," Cassie said with a smile. "I want to show you and Mom what Bucky learned today." She turned toward the puppy. "Bucky, sit," she said in a stern voice, using her finger to point to the ground. "Sit," she repeated when he simply looked at her.

He sat, tongue lolling to one side.

"Good boy," Cassie praised. "Now shake. Shake, Bucky." She held out her hand, and the dog lifted his paw into her hand.

"Good boy," she said again, pulling a dog treat out of her pocket. Bucky went a little crazy as soon as he smelled the treat, his entire body wiggling with excitement. Cassie gave him the treat, then looked up at them. "Isn't that awesome? He's so smart!"

"Amazing," she agreed, her mind still swirling over the idea of getting a closer look at the letter. "Hey, Cassie, guess what? Your dad invited us to have dinner tonight at the McNally Mansion so you can meet your aunts and uncles."

Cassie's eyes widened comically. "I have aunts and uncles?"

"You have lots of them," Jesse said dryly. "You can't meet them all today, they don't all live here, but hopefully someday soon. Tonight, you'll meet your Aunt Jazz and Uncle Dalton, and your Aunt Jemma and soon to be Uncle Garth, and your cousin Trey."

"I have a cousin?" Cassie began to bounce up and down with pure excitement. "That's so cool! I can't wait!"

In that moment, Carla knew that her daughter deserved this time to get to know the McNallys. As an only child herself, Carla knew how lonely it could feel, especially during holidays. Wasn't that one of the reasons she'd been so drawn to the McNallys all those years ago? The siblings had fought constantly, but at the same time, it had been clear that they would do anything for each other if needed.

Besides, she couldn't help thinking that maybe the letter Jesse's family had found in the attic would be the key to helping her mother get over being so angry with Jesse's father.

If Jesse's father had truly loved Lucy, it didn't make sense that he'd hurt her just because she was pregnant.

Her mother and Leon Tate must have that part of the story wrong. There must be something else that had transpired that fateful night.

10

Jesse picked up Carla at the grocery store at one forty-five. The house for rent wasn't very far, and he preferred to walk, especially since the town was full of tourists.

"Hey," Carla came out of the store, her brow furrowed with worry creases. "Hope you weren't waiting long."

"Not at all, what's wrong?" He didn't like seeing her looking stressed out and fought the urge to pull her into his arms.

"The usual." She waved a hand dismissively. "Nothing you can do."

"I don't know much about what it takes to run a grocery store, but I'm happy to listen."

"Tell me about this house you're looking at."

He wasn't fooled by her changing the subject. Whatever was bothering her, she didn't intend to tell him. Why, he had no idea. Didn't she trust him? The kiss they'd shared lingered in the back of his mind, and he'd been trying to think of a way to have some alone time with her.

But not like this, not when she was carrying the weight of work problems on her slim shoulders.

He only hoped that the issues were truly store related and not from that creep Dean Thomas. "It's small, but close to town, which is more important."

She arched a brow. "Seems like a guy who drives a little red Corvette enjoys the finer things in life."

"I like cars," he agreed, feeling defensive. He was secretly glad Carla had not seen his luxurious condo in Chicago. "But I'm not a snob. I'll take what I can get as long as I'm close to you and Cassie."

"We haven't exactly discussed co-custody arrangements," Carla said in a low voice. "I'm not sure how I'll feel about giving up the little time I have with Cassie."

"I don't want to take away from your time with her either." She was right, the co-custody arrangements wouldn't be easy. "But maybe she can spend some time with me while you're working?"

"That's fine, but come September she'll be in school all day. And you'll be traveling, too, for your job, right?"

"Yeah." He fell silent, realizing it wouldn't be easy to balance their crazy schedules. He wanted to tell Carla she didn't have to work at the grocery store if she didn't want to. That he made plenty of money and could support her and Cassie, but he sensed that idea wouldn't go over well.

The rental property was up ahead, and he found himself disappointed that it looked more run-down than it had on the website. The gray siding was old and cracked in a few places, and the white trim could have used a fresh coat of paint.

Maybe he was more high maintenance than he'd thought.

"This is it?" Carla eyed the property. "I know the owners,

Simon and Helen Kaplan. They live in Lansing and bought this place as a vacation home, gosh, must be almost ten years ago. They'd come often when their kids were younger but haven't used it much in the past few years. They've been renting it out for a month at a time during the summer."

"Yeah, it's not available until the first of September." He liked hearing the history of the place. "Wonder if they'd be interested in selling?"

"No clue."

They walked up the driveway. He glanced at his watch, taking note that it was already 2:00 p.m. "Where is Melanie Ryerson?"

"I think that's her now." Carla gestured to the vehicle coming to a stop at the side of the road in front of the house. A tall redhead slid out from behind the wheel, then crossed over to greet them with a smile.

"You must be Jesse McNally, I can tell, you resemble Jazz with your thick dark hair." Melanie shook his hand, then turned to Carla. "Nice to see you again, Carla."

"Likewise." Carla's smile didn't quite reach her eyes.

Jesse frowned. "You two know each other?"

"Not really," Carla said quickly. "Melanie's only been back for a couple of years."

"We went to high school together, although I was a year older," Melanie added. "People used to assume Carla was my younger sister because we both have red hair."

"I see." Although, he really didn't. There was something more going on here, but he wasn't sure what. He decided to probe Carla for more information later. "Do you have a key?"

"Of course. And the family renting the place for July have given permission for us to see the place while they're out." Melanie inserted the key in the lock and pushed the front door open. "Although I have to say, most realtors wouldn't be willing to come out on a holiday."

"I know, and thanks for doing this." Jesse gestured for Carla to go inside first. The interior was showing the same signs of wear and tear, but it was a cute place, decorated with a relaxed beach theme. "There are three bedrooms, right?"

"Correct." Melanie walked toward the kitchen area. "The place could use a little updating, but it's clean and functional."

He nodded in agreement as he poked his head into the bedrooms and the two bathrooms. With a little work, the place could be nice. Looking out through the wide living room window, you could even see a bit of the lake. Not a lot, but some.

"Do you think the Kaplans would be interested in selling?"

Melanie's eyes brightened with excitement. "I'm happy to ask them. Are you really interested in purchasing rather than renting? I know of another place, much bigger and nicer than this, that may be on the market soon."

He glanced at Carla, wishing Melanie hadn't mentioned a bigger, nicer place. Did he look like a snob? He didn't think so. He held Carla's gaze for a moment, but then she looked away. What did she think of the place? He had a feeling she wouldn't say much in front of Melanie.

"Depends on the price," he finally said. "But for now, I'm happy to rent this house starting the first of September."

"Great. I'll let the Kaplans know. And I'll see if they're interested in selling. Oh, and if not, just remember there are other properties, too." Melanie glanced between the two of them as if sensing she was the third wheel. "I'll be outside if you need anything."

When she left, he turned to Carla. "What do you think?"

"It's nice." Her tone was noncommittal.

"I'm surprised the Kaplans don't rent this place on their own, without an intermediary. Airbnbs are wildly successful."

She shrugged. "I don't know, some people are still old-fashioned. Not to mention, the realtor takes care of vetting the clients who rent the place and the cleaning between visits. The Kaplans don't have to do anything except let the money roll in."

"You don't like Melanie much, do you?"

Carla flushed and spread her hands. "It's not that I don't like her, we were never friends. That story about people considering us sisters is baloney. And she made snide comments when she returned to the area and found out I had a daughter but no husband."

"I see." And he didn't like it. "Is there another realtor I can work with instead?"

"There's only two of them, Melanie and an older guy by the name of Parker Stout. Parker likes to golf, so he's not around as much during the summer, and Melanie is more of a go-getter."

"I should have gone with Parker," he said with a sigh.

"It's fine." She dismissed his concern with a wave. "Really, Melanie is good at her job. Are you ready to go? Or was there more you wanted to see?"

"I'm good." He wished he'd thought to ask Carla for advice on which realtor to go with, rather than listening to Jazz. As they left, he glanced over his shoulder one more time at the warm interior of the place. It was easy to imagine living there, but not alone.

With Carla and Cassie. As a family.

RIDICULOUS TO FEEL nervous about having dinner with the McNallys. Carla decided to close the grocery store early, a rare occurrence. By three in the afternoon, things had slowed dramatically, so she figured that closing at five wouldn't cause a problem. She'd pulled produce from stock and put together a large salad to bring to the dinner party as well. Then she told her mother the news.

"You what?" Her mother's voice rose with indignation as if Carla had done something unforgivable. "You can't just close the store early. What if someone stops by to pick something up?"

"They'll come back tomorrow." She tried not to cave beneath the weight of her mother's guilt trip. Normally the store only closed early on Christmas Eve and for all of Christmas Day. The other holidays they were open, even on New Year's.

A schedule Carla hadn't messed with, until today.

"Why would you do such a thing?" Her mother looked genuinely agitated. "People in the town depend on the store being open when they need something."

"You're making a big deal out of nothing, Mom. The place was quiet. There wasn't a single customer between four and five o'clock." She cleared her throat, then added, "Cassie and I have plans for dinner tonight. In fact, we're already running late."

"Plans? With Jesse McNally?"

"Yes." She turned away, hoping to avoid an argument. "Cassie? Time to go!"

"Coming!" Cassie sounded excited.

"I can't believe . . ." her mother started, but Carla held up a hand.

"Don't ruin this for Cassie. She deserves this time with her father. It will be nice for her to establish a good relationship with him."

Her mother clamped her lips together, sensing Carla's bitterness related to her own relationship, or lack thereof, with her dad. Ironic that she now supported bonding time for Jesse and Cass. Her mother's expression remained closed and shuttered as they left.

Carla set the salad in the back seat. She hated being at odds with her mother and hoped the letter written by Justin to Lucy may be the key.

"I can't wait to meet my cousin."

"I'm glad. Although, you should know he's a lot younger than you are." She tried to remember the last time she'd seen Jemma and Trey. Probably before Jazz and Dalton's wedding.

"I know. Dad told me Trey is going to be four soon. But I don't mind."

Carla drove her old reliable Honda down the highway toward the McNallys' B&B. As she pulled into the driveway, Cassie gasped with admiration. "It's so big!"

"Just remember, it's a bed and breakfast," she warned. "And there are probably guests staying there."

"I know." Cassie had her door open before Carla had put the gear shift into park. Shaking her head wryly, she shut down the engine and got out of the car. She rescued the salad from the back seat, then approached the large, yellow two-story house.

The front door opened, revealing a smiling Jemma McNally. "It's great to see you both, please come in."

"It's nice to see you, too." She held up the large bowl. "I brought salad."

"Wonderful. Here, I'll take that for you. Come on

through to the backyard, that's where the rest of the family is."

"Wow. It's so beautiful," Cassie said, looking around the great room with wide eyes. Carla had to agree. A Cliffs of Moher painting hung over the fireplace flanked by tall antique-looking silver candlesticks. Deep cherry-wood furniture made the room look regal and comfy at the same time. A curved, elegant staircase led the way to the second floor, where Carla assumed the bedrooms were located. She'd had only been inside the mansion once or twice during that summer with Jesse, and never upstairs. They'd always spent their time together outside.

"Better than I imagined," Cass added.

Her stomach knotted with nerves as Jemma led the way through the large kitchen and dining areas. The white gazebo overlooked the lake. Jemma opened the French doors leading outside, then stood off to the side encouraging Carla and Cassie to go out first.

Jesse hurried over from the gazebo, and for a moment, she thought she saw a hint of nervousness in his eyes, too. "Hi, Carla, Cassie. Welcome. I hope you both like barbequed ribs, potato salad, and grilled corn on the cob."

"Sounds great. I brought a green salad, too." Carla swept her gaze over the group sitting on deck chairs inside the gazebo, lingering for a moment on Jazz.

"Carla!" Jazz hurried forward and engulfed her in a hug. "I'm so glad you could make it."

"Me, too," she managed. That summer they'd been close despite their couple year age difference, but that had changed drastically once she'd gone away to college.

Upon returning home, Carla had done everything possible to avoid the McNally family. But now, she couldn't help but wonder how things might have been different if she hadn't.

Would Jazz have guessed who Cassie's father was? Would Jesse have known about his daughter sooner?

Jesse performed introductions. Cassie was thrilled to meet Trey and the Goldendoodle puppy, Goldie.

"Do you think Bucky and Goldie are brother and sister?" Cassie asked.

"They are," Jemma confirmed. "I'm fairly certain all the puppies found good homes."

"Too bad, I would love one." Cassie looked disappointed.

After a few minutes, the last of her nervousness fled beneath the warm welcome. Jesse pulled her down to sit beside him under the gazebo where she could easily watch as Cass and Trey played with Goldie.

The food was delicious and plentiful. She smirked when Jesse went for seconds.

When there was a lull in the conversation, she tried to think of a way to ask about the letter. Thankfully, Jesse sensed her thoughts.

"Jemma, do you mind if we show Carla Dad's letter?"

"Sure, why not?" Jemma jumped up from her seat next to Garth. "I have to take the leftovers in anyway."

"I'll help," Carla offered.

"Nope, you and Cassie are our guests. Stay here, I'll be back in a jiff."

"Did Jesse fill you in on the history between our family and the Tates?" Jazz asked.

She nodded. "Yes, and you should know that my parents were friends of the Tates too."

"Oh." Jazz grimaced. "I'm sure that means your parents are on their side."

"My mom is, yes." She cleared her throat, trying not to

look at Jesse. "My dad died nine years ago."

There was a moment of silence as Jazz, Dalton, and Deputy Garth Lewis digested that bit of information.

"Here you go," Jemma said, returning to the gazebo with an old, yellowed slip of paper. "Be careful, it's fragile."

"I will." Carla quickly read through the brief note, then read it again for a second time. It was amazing how the sadness and grief leapt off the page.

"We know J is for Justin," Jesse said. "According to Mrs. Cromwell, our Dad and Lucy were a hot item back then."

"My mom said the same thing." Carla hesitated, then decided to share the rest. "My mom and Leon Tate both blame your father for Lucy's death."

"Because he was driving the boat that night," Jazz said with a nod.

"Not just that." Carla wondered if her mother would forgive her for breaching her confidence, but she decided they needed to know. "My mom was Lucy's best friend. She says Lucy was pregnant."

"Pregnant?" both Jazz and Jemma echoed in unison while Jesse let out a low whistle.

"That explains a lot," he said in a low voice.

"Wouldn't the ME's report show that?" Jazz asked.

"It should, but we haven't seen the report for ourselves," Jemma pointed out. "Maybe it's time we take a look at it."

"How can we get it?" Jazz asked.

"I'm not sure," Jemma admitted.

"I know this letter is yours, but I'd like to show it to my mother," Carla said. "She needs to know how your father really felt about Lucy."

There was another long moment of silence before Jazz spoke up. "Are you saying your mom thinks our dad hurt Lucy on purpose?"

"I'm afraid so." Carla shook her head. "Terrible, right? Isn't it time the Tate family learned the truth?"

"I doubt old Leon will believe it," Jemma said with a resigned sigh. "I think he likes hating us."

"Why not take a picture of the letter with your phone for now? We'll show your mom the original later," Jesse suggested.

Carla snapped the picture, wondering what her mother would think. As the sun hovered low over the lake to the west, the conversation veered from the past to the present. She enjoyed hearing Garth and Jemma's wedding plans. They'd picked the middle weekend in August to get married and expressed their hope that the rest of the siblings would attend.

"Let's take a walk," Jesse suggested, pulling her out of her chair.

"What about Cassie?"

"Jemma and Jazz will keep an eye on her."

She felt self-conscious as the two couples watched them leave. Jesse's hand was warm around hers. They wandered aimlessly along the shoreline when he abruptly stopped.

"Carla." He took her other hand so he could look deep into her eyes. "I want you to know how much I care about you."

Her heart did a crazy double beat in her chest. "I care about you, too."

His gaze searched hers, then he drew her close. "I think I know why I haven't been seriously involved with anyone over the past nine years," he said in a low, gravelly tone.

"You do?" Her voice was breathless.

"Because none of them were you." He slowly lowered his mouth to hers, kissing her softly at first, then with the passion and desire she remembered from long ago.

11

———

He wanted, needed Carla in a way he hadn't felt in nine years. Kissing her was so much better now than it had been before.

And he never wanted to stop.

When they both needed to breathe, he lifted his head and cradled her close, resting his cheek on her hair. It felt so right, so perfect to hold her in his arms.

"We shouldn't do this," Carla whispered.

Jesse tried not to sigh. "Why not? I care about you, Carla."

She pushed away from him. "Like you did the blonde?"

"I told you I barely remember her." He tried to keep the edge from his tone. "I know it's my fault. I mentioned getting together over homecoming, then never followed up on the invite. And I can admit, I went a little crazy those early weeks of college. Madison is known to be a party school. But it wasn't long until I turned my back on all of that. I buckled down and worked hard to maintain my grades. I graduated with honors."

"I know, and I'm happy for you." Carla hunched her

shoulders and turned to stare out over the water. "I just don't think we should rush into anything."

He wasn't sure what she meant by that. Did she not feel the same way toward him as she once did? His heart squeezed in his chest, and he wondered if this was how Carla had felt watching him with the blonde he couldn't even remember.

Especially when he hadn't even followed through on his invite to have her come up for a visit. No wonder she was so upset with him.

"Carla, I don't want to rush you, but tell me this—how much of your resistance is because you don't care about me the way you used to versus your mother's deep hatred for every one of the McNallys?"

She didn't answer for a long moment, still staring off at the sunset. "The letter your dad wrote to Lucy should help my mother back off and get over some of her hatred toward your father, but if you want me to be honest with you"—she paused, then turned to face him—"it's me. I don't want to be hurt the way I was before."

He wanted to kick his younger self in the seat of the pants all the way to Kalamazoo. "I'm sorry I hurt you. That was never my intention."

Her smile was sad. "But the end result is still the same."

A flutter of panic curled in his belly. "Please, Carla, give me a second chance. I am not the same irresponsible guy you spent the summer with nine years ago."

"And I'm not the same naïve girl," she responded. "I have Cassie's future to think about. Any relationship between us will have an impact on her, and I don't want her getting her hopes up that we're going to be some sort of cozy family."

Since that was exactly what he wanted, he held his tongue and tried to help her understand. "I don't want to hurt Cassie either. Or your mother for that matter. I just want a chance with you."

"I think you're letting the heat of summer cloud your judgment," she said on a sigh. "Right now, you're off work and have all day to spend with me and Cass packing picnics, taking boat rides. But this isn't reality, Jesse. Once you're off traveling for work and I'm still managing the store, you'll see that all of this"—she waved an impatient hand—"isn't real. Just like our summer together nine years ago wasn't real."

"It was real to me." The minute the words left his mouth, he wanted to call them back.

"You stopped calling, stopped writing, and didn't return my phone call at the beginning of October." She ticked the items on the fingers of one hand. "And when I came to visit you as you'd mentioned, you weren't there for me because you'd moved on. That is the reality, Jesse. Not the young love we once shared, but the harsh aftermath."

Meaning leaving her pregnant and alone with a baby daughter.

"We were young," he agreed. "And I was selfish, focused only on my future." A degree Carla hadn't been able to obtain, which really bothered him. "But that's what I'm trying to say. I'm not that same guy. And I like to think that if I'd known about Cassie, I would have stepped up and taken responsibility."

"Yes, well, that's all water under the bridge." She glanced past him to where the McNallys were still gathered beneath the gazebo. "We should get back. It's getting late, and I have to work early in the morning."

"Okay." He agreed, because really, what choice did he have? Carla wasn't on vacation the way he was, which sort of proved her point. This idyllic time they had wasn't how things would be every day in the future.

Just the thought of flying home to Chicago on Sunday filled him with dread. He wasn't ready to go. To leave. Spending time away from Carla and Cassie would be unbearable.

As they strolled back to the B&B, he thought about contacting his partner again. Brian had been relieved when Jesse had fixed the Trojan horse virus that infected their software. But he hadn't been as thrilled to hear of Jesse's plan to relocate to McNally Bay. Brian had pointed out all the issues Jesse was already aware of, that traveling out of a smaller airport wouldn't be nearly as convenient as Chicago and that they still needed to meet monthly to go over their operating income statements.

Small hurdles in his opinion. Brian needed to know that his traveling days were going to be far less than they had been. If Jesse could swing it financially, he'd prefer to cut his travel time in half.

Brian wouldn't like it, but too bad.

A few years ago, they had talked about the possibility of bringing another employee into their company. Clearly, the time to do that was now. Their services were still in high demand, and there would be more than enough income to go around.

With a sense of relief, he decided to broach the subject with Brian as soon as he returned to Chicago.

Taking action, doing something positive was the best way to prove to Carla how much he still cared about her.

How much he loved her.

~

It took all of Carla's willpower not to sprint back to the

gazebo, sweep Cassie in her arms, and hightail it out of there as fast as she could.

Too much. It was all just too much.

Jesse's kisses had a way of messing with her mind. She couldn't think rationally around him, and she needed to keep a cool head.

She'd told herself she wasn't going to be sucked in by his charm and charisma the way she had nine years ago. Yet one kiss and her resolve had drifted off over the lake like an early morning fog.

"Hey, Cass, it's time to go," she called as they reached the gazebo.

"Aw, Mom, we're just about to make s'mores! And the fireworks are going to be starting soon."

She sighed, having forgotten all about the fireworks. And she should have anticipated dessert.

Jemma looked distressed. "I'm sorry, I should have asked you first, but the grill is still hot enough to roast marshmallows. And the fireworks will start at dark."

"It's fine. Sure, we can stay long enough for you to make a few s'mores and watch the fireworks." Just what she needed, more time to sit beside Jesse.

"Thanks, Mom!" Cassie and Trey both had found long sticks to use for their marshmallows, and her daughter was helping her young cousin with putting them on the end of the stick. "Okay, now come stand by me, Trey. Not too close, it's going to feel hot."

Watching her daughter care for Trey was humbling. It only proved what she'd already known, it wasn't much fun being an only child.

"She's a good kid," Jesse said softly. "You did a wonderful job raising her."

The job wasn't over by a long shot, but she appreciated

his comment. "Thanks. And you need to know my mom helped me out a lot. She helped with childcare when Cassie was young, gave me a job at the store." She sent him a sidelong look. "Something you need to keep in mind. Cassie is a well-adjusted kid primarily because of my mom's support."

Jesse nodded thoughtfully. "I'm sorry to hear about your dad's passing. What happened?"

She hesitated. "Heart attack."

Jesse winced. "I'm sorry. I'm sure that wasn't easy for either one of you."

"It wasn't." And that was the biggest understatement of the decade. This wasn't the time or the place to talk about exactly how and when her father had died.

"See, then when the marshmallow is golden brown, we put it on the graham cracker and square of chocolate like this." Cassie showed Trey. "Then we make a sandwich."

"Yummy," Trey said, reaching for a s'more.

"Careful, it might still be hot." Cassie handed the first s'more to Trey, then made one for herself.

The fireworks began a short while later. They all moved out from under the gazebo so they could watch the display high over Lake Michigan.

Sitting on the grass with Cassie between them was bittersweet. She was glad to share this with Cassie but wished her mother could have been there, too.

As soon as the fireworks ended, with a rousing round of applause, Carla stood. "Okay, Cass, it's time to go."

"Aw, Mom, I want to stay." The familiar stubborn glint flashed in her daughter's eye. "Trey is still up, and he's younger than me."

"I can bring her home later," Jesse offered.

"No." She glared at him for a moment, silently warning him to back off. "I'm sorry, but it's time to go. Thank Aunt

Jemma, Uncle Garth, Aunt Jazz, and Uncle Dalton for the party."

Cassie glared at her for a moment, then relented. "Thank you for the party," she said. "I'm so glad to know I have aunts and uncles and a cousin!"

"We're thrilled to have you, too." Jemma pulled Cassie into a quick hug, then Jazz did the same. "I hope we'll see you again very soon, Cassie."

Cass looked as if she was walking the plank of a pirate ship as she came toward Carla. Really, the kid might have a career in acting based on the exaggerated drooping shoulders and sad face.

"Oh, don't forget your salad bowl." Jemma quickly picked it up off the table. "There isn't much left I'm afraid, but thanks again for bringing it."

"The party was fun." She liked Jemma and Jazz a lot. Under different circumstances, they could easily grow into close friends. "Thanks again for inviting us."

"You're both welcome any time," Jazz assured her. "Family takes care of family, right?"

Her smile was sad as she thought of her mother. And her strained relationship with her father. "Right."

Jesse walked her and Cassie around the house to the parking area in front of the house. "Would you be willing to have lunch with me again tomorrow?"

"Um, sure." She didn't want to say no in front of Cassie. "At the diner?"

"No, I was thinking we'd go for a drive out of town. Have another picnic."

She wanted to refuse but understood that Jesse's week of vacation time was almost up. Why not enjoy it? "Sounds good."

"Can I invite my friend Alecia?" Cassie asked. "And can we go swimming this time?"

"Sure," Jesse agreed. Then he backtracked and added, "If your mom says it's okay."

"It's fine." A little late, she thought with a sigh. Jesse had to understand he couldn't keep undermining her authority. Cassie was a good kid now, but those dreaded teenage years weren't that far off.

"Great, I'll pick you up at the store at noon." Jesse opened the car door for her. "Thanks for coming."

She set the mostly empty salad bowl on the back seat, then slid in behind the wheel. With a little wave, she backed out of the McNally driveway and drove home.

Cassie chatted about Trey and Goldie and how lucky her cousin was to have a dog of his own, once again putting in a bid for a puppy. Even being reminded of how she was earning money to take care of Bucky didn't seem to distract her.

Her daughter's mood didn't improve once they were home. Cassie stomped off into the bathroom, muttering that it wasn't fair she had to go to bed earlier than her not-yet four-year-old cousin. And her mother wasn't speaking to her either, pretending to be engrossed in a murder mystery when Carla knew full well she hadn't turned a single page since they'd come inside.

Once she'd convinced Cassie to brush her teeth and get ready for bed, she approached her mom with the phone.

"I have something to show you."

For a moment, she thought her mother wasn't going to respond, but she finally lifted her gaze. "What?"

"The McNallys found a letter in the attic that was written by Justin to Lucy." She held out the phone with the letter blown up on the screen. "I think you should read it."

Her mother stared at the phone as if it were a huge hairy spider, but curiosity finally won out over disgust, and she took the device and read the short note.

"How do you know it's real?" her mom finally asked.

"I'll get the original to show you, but trust me, it's old and brittle, the ink faded on the page. Jemma found the letter tucked into the family Bible in the attic. They have no reason to lie, Mom. They didn't know anything about Lucy or her death until they stumbled across the letter."

Her mother thrust the phone back into her hand. "Have you told Jesse what happened to your father?"

"Not yet." Carla frowned. "So that's it? You see with your own eyes how much Justin cared about Lucy, but you still want to hate Jesse?"

Her mother jumped up from the chair, the book falling to the floor with a soft thud. "He's the reason your dad is gone," she spat in a low, furious tone. "I'm just supposed to forgive him? For everything he's done?"

"Yes." Carla faced her mother. "You are. Because my having Cassie isn't all Jesse's fault, and frankly, this ridiculous grudge against the entire family has to stop."

"Don't tell me what to do, young lady." Her mother didn't back down. "My feelings are my business."

"So, you hate me now, too? Because I was the one who was there when Dad died. My telling him about being pregnant caused his heart attack. I was the one who tried to do CPR to keep him alive. If you're going to hate Jesse because of the role he played, then you must feel the same way about me."

"I'm going to bed." Her mother pushed past her, but Carla grabbed her hand to stop her.

"This is as much about Cassie as anything," she insisted. "Cassie is a McNally by blood. She has an extended family, including a young cousin that she's thrilled about. Don't do this, Mom. Don't keep up this level of hate. It will only turn against you in the long run."

Her mother went still, before roughly jerking away. She left the room, leaving Carla standing there feeling helpless.

Her hope of turning her mother's attitude around was proving futile. Carla knew she got her own redheaded stubbornness from her mother, but this was ridiculous. It was as if the older woman refused to listen to reason.

Carla was so upset she couldn't relax, much less try to go to sleep. She slipped outside and began to walk in an effort to burn off the anger, sadness, and regret.

Without realizing it, she found herself down on Main Street where dozens of people were still milling about, many having watched the firework display and were either heading home or heading to the Bombay Pub and Grill located at the west end of the street, catty-corner from Gino's.

Someone roughly grabbed her arm, and her stomach knotted when she saw Dean Thomas standing beside her. Well, he was swaying more than he was standing, and she wrinkled her nose at the stench of alcohol seeping from his pores.

"Can't even say hi anymore?" Dean slurred his words to the point she had trouble understanding him.

"I didn't see you." She tried to shake off his grasp, but his fingers tightened painfully on her forearm. "Let me go, Dean. You're drunk."

"Had a couple of shots at Bombay," he admitted. More than a couple by the looks of him. Under the light from the streetlamp, she could see his eyes were red and bloodshot.

"Let me go," she repeated, raising her voice. She wasn't really afraid of him; there were plenty of people around.

"You need to move on, Dean. Find someone else. A woman who can care about you the way you deserve."

"I loved you, Carla." He still hadn't released her, and she was getting super annoyed with him. "How could you turn your back on me?"

There was no point in arguing with a drunk, so she tried to pry his fingers off her arm. "Let me go or I'll call the police."

He staggered, and the shifting of his weight caused him to lean closer. She tried not to gag at the horrible stench of his breath.

She wished Jesse was there with her to help deal with Dean. But he was back at the McNallys' B&B.

Anger bubbled up inside her. "Get away from me!" She brought her knee up to his groin, then shoved him as hard as she could. He let her go, bending over with a low moan, then went down, hitting the cement sidewalk with a jarring thud.

"Hey, are you all right?" A woman she didn't recognize came over to her side. "Should we call the police?"

"I'm fine." She rubbed the spot on her forearm where Dean had clung to her, knowing she'd have bruises in the morning. "But yeah, I think we should call the police. Not only did he try to assault me, but he's drunk and shouldn't be driving."

"I'm on it." The tourist pulled out her cell phone and dialed 911.

Deputy Waldorf was there in less than five minutes. She took Carla's statement, along with Naomi's who was the bystander who'd come to her rescue. Hearing the same story from both of them had Deputy Waldorf hauling Dean into her squad to take him to jail.

Carla watched them drive away, glad he wouldn't be a problem for a while.

But when he got out of jail? She shivered. If he was mad at her now, he'd likely be furious with her once he'd sobered up.

And she knew it was highly likely Dean would take his anger out on her daughter once school started in the fall.

12

———

Jesse woke up Friday morning, feeling depressed that he only had two more days to spend with Carla and Cassie before he needed to head back Chicago.

He didn't want to go. Deep down, he couldn't help feeling that if he left, he'd lose some of the ground he'd recently gained with Carla. Not to mention, he liked seeing his daughter every day.

Could he stay? He turned the idea over in his mind. Jemma had assured him the master suite in the B&B was his for as long as he needed it. The arrangement wasn't perfect, but it was better than being a hundred miles away. Why not take her up on the offer?

Since he was planning to move to McNally Bay at the end of the summer, there was no reason to wait. The house he'd hoped to rent wouldn't be available until September, but in the meantime, he could still travel in and out of McNally Bay while living in the B&B. He could store his stuff in a corner of the massive four-car garage. The place was roomy enough, Jazz kept her truck parked at the

Stevenson house, so Jemma's van was the only vehicle currently using the space.

He'd have to sell his condo, but that shouldn't be too difficult. He didn't care if he made a huge profit, he had plenty of equity in the place.

As he enjoyed Jemma's full Irish breakfast, he began to make arrangements. First, he contacted Brian, letting his partner know Jesse wasn't returning to Chicago on Sunday as previously planned. Brian didn't answer his phone, so he ended up leaving a message, assuring Brian that he'd still work hard to make their business successful but that he needed to do this. Once that task was done, he decided to make a list of things he'd need shipped to McNally Bay.

Mostly clothes and personal items, but there was also the issue of his two vehicles. The owner of the garage that had taken care of his damaged Corvette called to let him know his car was ready to be picked up. Jesse thanked him, then hung up. As much as he loved driving the Corvette, he knew how impractical it was.

It was a two-seater, which meant he wouldn't be able to drive both Carla and Cassie around at the same time. And really, what was the point? It was fun to drive, but a better option would be to trade the Vette in for a sedan. Something Carla could also drive, since he already had an SUV that he drove primarily over the winter months. Her car looked as if it was on its last spark plug. He wasn't sure it would last the upcoming winter.

Maybe he should fly back to Chicago, just to pick up the SUV and to put the Vette up for sale. He could turn right around and drive the SUV back to McNally Bay.

Lost in his thoughts, he didn't hear Jazz come up beside him. "Don't tell me you're working again."

"What? Oh, no." He waited until she'd finished filling his

coffee mug. "Actually, I'm trying to figure out a plan to move my stuff here, sooner than later."

"Really? Oh, Jesse, that's wonderful news!" Jazz set down her coffee pot to give him an enthusiastic hug, her green eyes shimmering with tears. "Jemma will be thrilled."

"Yeah, well, I haven't worked out all the kinks yet." He gestured to his computer. "I'm making a list. I'll need a ride to the airport to fly home and pick up my car."

"The Corvette has been fixed? That's great news."

"Not that car, my SUV. I'm selling the Vette since it's not a family car."

"Wow, that's good news, too. Cassie seems like a great kid," Jazz said with a smile. "Although, I wish we would have known about her sooner. Carla and I were close that summer. It hurts that she hadn't confided in me."

"Don't blame her too much. She didn't know about the pregnancy until she was halfway through her first semester of college. And I casually mentioned her coming up for homecoming weekend but never actually formalized any plans with her." Ironic how he was defending what Carla had done. "In the end, she came up to find me that homecoming weekend in time to see me kissing some blonde that I don't remember."

"Ouch." Jazz winced. "I'm sure that was rough."

"Yeah. And it's obvious she'd been keeping Cassie's parentage a secret because of the animosity her mother has against us." He waved a hand impatiently. "None of that matters anymore. I intend to move forward from here, being a part of Cassie's life. Her mother will just have to get over it."

"And Carla?" Jazz grinned. "I can tell you still care about her."

"I do. Very much." He frowned. "Unfortunately, I don't think she feels the same way."

"She does. I witnessed your kiss on the beach; the passion was enough to spark a wildfire. I'm sure she's just being cautious."

Since Carla had said exactly that, he nodded. "Maybe. I need to convince her that I'm not the same guy who'd gone a little crazy during my first semester of college. I've changed, hopefully for the better."

"Well, moving to McNally Bay is the best way to prove you're serious," Jazz said. "That's a huge first step."

Before he could say anything more, additional guests came into the dining area. Jazz immediately went over to greet them, chatting about breakfast options while filling coffee cups.

He turned his attention back to his checklist. After checking available flights out of Kalamazoo, he paid to change his ticket to an earlier flight. It would mean getting up at four in the morning, but it was worth it. If he moved quickly, he could drive the SUV the just under two hundred miles back to McNally Bay in time for dinner. The traffic going through Chicago and Gary, Indiana, would slow him down some, but he thought it was still doable.

Satisfied, he finished his breakfast. He caught a glimpse of a scathing review left by Avery and Arch related to the work he'd done for them. He wished he could delete it, but obviously he couldn't. Ignoring the awful review, he quickly shut down his computer. It didn't matter, they had other clients who'd appreciated their help.

He wanted to finalize the details of the picnic outing for that afternoon. He planned on asking Daisy to make the food again, knowing Jemma would be busy with her guests. There was a rehearsal tonight for the gazebo wedding scheduled for late afternoon on Saturday. All the rooms in the B&B were taken by the wedding party, most of which had come in Thursday afternoon to stay the entire three nights of the holiday weekend.

He headed to Daisy's Diner to make arrangements with Daisy, who was happy to help him out. It was nice to see how the locals supported each other.

As he was about to leave, he saw Cassie walking toward him with Bucky on his leash. "Hi, Dad." She greeted him with a wide grin, and he knew he'd never tire of hearing her call him Dad. "What time should I tell Alecia to be ready?"

"Eleven thirty. Can you and Alecia meet us at your mom's grocery store? She probably can't get off until noon, but as soon as she's finished, we'll head out."

Cassie nodded. "We're bringing our swimming suits and towels."

"Good plan." He'd rented the boat with the idea of allowing the girls plenty of time to swim in the bay. He made a mental note to buy some flotation devices and tried to think of a way to convince Carla to let her guard down enough to enjoy the water. "See you in a couple of hours, okay?"

"Okay." Cassie took Bucky back inside up to the second story apartment over the diner where Daisy lived.

Of all the places he looked for flotation devices, he hadn't expected to find them in the novelty section of Carla's grocery store. There was no sign of her when he went in to pick up what he needed.

"Did you hear about Dean Thomas getting arrested?"

Instantly on alert, Jesse tucked the inflatable rafts under his arm and turned toward the sound of Betty Cromwell's voice. "No, why? What happened?"

Mrs. Cromwell's eyes gleamed. There was nothing she

liked better than spreading news. "Drunk as a skunk, he grabbed Carla right there on Main Street in front of several witnesses and wouldn't let go."

A red haze of anger veiled his vision as he imagined what Carla must have suffered. "When?" His voice was thick with emotion.

"Last night, but don't worry, Carla kneed him in the groin and shoved him down to the ground, just like Wonder Woman," Mrs. Cromwell continued. "Then Deputy Waldorf hauled him to jail. Heard by the time he sobered up he was real sorry about causing a scene. You know, him being the elementary school principal and all."

Jesse was still trying to wrap his mind around the fact that this had all transpired just last night, after he'd dropped Carla and Cassie off at her mother's house. What was Carla doing on Main Street anyway? Had she purposefully gone out to meet with Thomas? Or with someone else?

And more importantly, why hadn't she called him?

CARLA FINISHED her work in record time, partially because she'd delegated some of the inventory responsibilities to her senior cashier, Sheryl Watts. The single mother of two teenage children didn't seem to mind the additional responsibilities. In fact, she offered to take on any other tasks Carla needed her to.

It occurred to her that Sheryl may be the perfect candidate to be an assistant manager. Sheryl had roots here in McNally Bay and was doing her best to support her family. Carla actually felt guilty for not thinking of her before now.

Before she could talk herself out of it, she asked Sheryl to meet with her in the office for a few minutes. Her senior cashier looked wary at first, nervously twisting her hands together.

"Sheryl, how would you like a raise and a promotion to Assistant Manager?"

The older woman's jaw dropped. "Me? Are you sure? I don't have a fancy business degree or anything like Richard did."

"That business degree didn't help me much since he didn't stay," Carla pointed out. And the man had been far too arrogant anyway. "Listen, I can't do all of this alone anymore, and you've proven to be a great help. If you're interested, I'll give you a ten percent raise starting Monday."

"Oh, yes! I'm very interested." Sheryl impulsively gave Carla a quick hug. "Thank you so much. I won't let you down."

"I have faith in you, don't worry." Carla glanced at her watch, knowing she needed to meet Jesse and the girls within the next thirty minutes. "We'll work out a schedule later, okay? I think we can break up the hours so that we work alternate late shifts and weekends."

"That sounds good." Sheryl clasped her hands together. "A ten percent raise! I can't wait to tell the boys."

"You've earned it," Carla assured her. "Now go on, get back to work. I'll be off-site for a few hours again this afternoon, but you know you can reach me on my cell phone."

"I won't bother you unless it's a crisis," Sheryl promised. "Thanks again."

As Sheryl hurried off, Carla felt as if a giant weight had lifted off her shoulders. Granted, the raise and shared responsibilities would put a dent in their profit margin, but at the moment it seemed a small price to pay in order to have more time with Cassie.

And with Jesse. She'd be lying if she didn't admit that

she was looking forward to spending the afternoon with him. It wasn't smart, she was growing far too attached to the guy who'd once stolen her heart and then blasted it into tiny pieces.

But since when were feelings logical? Since never.

She pushed the unwelcome thoughts aside and focused on finishing the last bit of work before heading out for an afternoon of relaxing in the sun.

True to his word, Jesse was waiting outside by Jemma's old van with both Cassie and Alecia dressed in their swimsuits and cover-ups.

"Guess the girls are swimming."

"Mom, I brought your swimming suit too, in case you want to cool off in the lake." Cassie beamed with excitement. "And Dad bought air mattresses for us."

"Really?" She wondered where he'd gotten them but decided not to ask. "Well okay, then, let's go."

"Would you like to stop at your place to change?" Jesse opened the van door so the girls could climb in the back. "I don't mind. The temperature is supposed to get up to ninety-six degrees."

She almost refused, but then glanced down at her usual work clothes. Shorts and a T-shirt would be so much more comfortable. Not that she intended to do any swimming. She was too self-conscious about the five pounds of baby weight she'd never shed after Cassie was born. "That would be great."

Jesse nodded, then glanced down at her right wrist. He caught her hand in his, examining the bruises that Dean had left there. "I want to punch him in the face for this." Jesse's voice was low. "I wish you would have called me."

"For you to come punch him? Deputy Waldorf would have had to arrest you, too." She shouldn't have been surprised he'd heard the news. "It's fine, and I didn't call you because there was nothing you could do about it. Deputy Waldorf arrested Dean, and that was enough for me. Let's go, okay? I want to enjoy the sunshine."

He gently squeezed her hand, then released it. He opened her car door, then jogged around to get in behind the wheel.

Thankfully, her mother wasn't home when she ran inside to change. Probably spending time with Leon Tate, telling him about the note Jemma had found in the McNally attic. She'd really hoped her mother would let go of her old anger, but so far, that hadn't happened.

Whatever. Carla refused to let her mother's grudge ruin her day. She felt carefree and lighthearted, knowing the store was in good hands with Sheryl.

Jesse hauled the large cooler to the boat, leaving the girls and Carla to bring their floaties and bags of clothing and towels.

Carla unhooked the rope holding the boat to the pier and pushed off. Jesse pulled away from shore, keeping an eye on the dozens of boaters out on the lake.

It was far more crowded than it had been the last time they'd come out, and Carla knew that meant the holiday weekend was in full swing. Jesse took them for a fast ride, making the girls screech with joy and fear, before turning around and heading back to a secluded area of the bay.

"Okay, I think this is a perfect place for you girls to swim," he announced, throwing a large anchor overboard. "The water is about ten feet deep here, so you need to be careful."

"I know how to swim," Cassie protested. "I don't want to wear my life jacket."

"Me either," Alecia added. "I'm a good swimmer."

"I know, but the water is much cooler than you're used to." He pinned them with a stern look. "Okay, you can take off your life jackets to use the floaties, but I don't want either of you to stay in for too long. When I say it's time to get out, you both get out. Understand?"

Carla hid a smile as the girls pouted for a moment, then agreed to follow the rules.

Jesse tossed the two air mattresses off first, then gestured for the girls to follow. The cold water caused a surprised squeal from both of them, but they quickly climbed onto an air mattress and stretched out.

"This is fun," Alecia declared. "Thanks for inviting me."

Carla stretched out on the boat with a sigh, thinking the same thing.

"Hey, I have some news," Jesse said.

She turned toward him. "Is it something I'll eventually hear from Betty Cromwell?"

He laughed, and the sound made her smile. "Yeah, probably, but I thought you should hear it first."

Her pulse spiked, although she did her best not to let it show on her face. "Okay, spill."

"I'm moving to McNally Bay on Sunday." He grinned and waited expectantly.

The statement took her by surprise. "I thought the Kaplan place wasn't available until September?"

"My sisters invited me to stay at the B&B until I can officially take over the house. And I might keep looking for someplace else anyway." His gaze seemed to bore into hers. "Somehow, I expected you to be happy about this."

"I am," she hastened to reassure him. "Truly. But Jesse, we haven't really discussed this. Or anything related to how we'll work things out between us with Cass. My mother still doesn't like you, and I'm not sure how or when that will change. I don't know, it feels a little like you're jumping the gun."

He frowned, and she knew this wasn't going the way he'd planned. "How is it jumping the gun? I told you I wanted to be a part of Cassie's life. That I wanted to live here in the area. Just because I'm moving sooner than September doesn't mean anything has to dramatically change right this instant. We can keep taking things a step at a time."

She smiled, feeling relieved that he wasn't trying to rush things. "You're right, Cassie's well-being is far more important than anything else. Okay, I'm happy to know you're moving this weekend. What does your business partner have to say about it?"

"I left him a message, and he returned my call an hour or so later. Brian is fine, gave me his blessing, and promised we'd work things out. He even suggested we could use Skype to do our operational meetings."

"That's good to hear." She could tell Jesse was relieved his partner was being supportive. She glanced over to where the girls were swimming in the lake, both stretched out on their air mattresses, gazing up at the cloudless sky. "We should probably bring them in to eat."

"Girls," Jesse called. "Ten minutes till lunch."

"Aw, we're not cold at all," Cass protested.

"Ten minutes," Jesse repeated.

Carla turned her attention to the cooler. This time it looked as if Daisy had packed cold cuts, breads, and cheese along with fresh fruit and fat brownies for dessert. There were soft drinks and water inside, and she helped herself to a water. The sun was hot, and she found herself considering a brief swim.

"Cassie!" Alecia's scream ripped through the air. She glanced over to the girls and saw an empty air mattress a split second before she noticed Cassie floating bonelessly facedown in the water.

"Cassie!" Without thinking, she ran to the edge of the boat and levered herself up and over into the water.

Shockingly cold water stole her breath, but she swiped the water from her face and forced herself to swim toward her daughter, hoping and praying she wouldn't be too late.

13

———

Jesse heard Carla's shout at the same time he noticed Cassie floating limply in the water, her slender body rising and falling with each wave. His heart lodged in his throat. Carla was several strokes ahead of him, but he quickly followed. He was strong, but Carla still managed to beat him to their daughter.

When she reached Cassie, the girl abruptly popped upright with a saucy grin, wiping the water from her face with her hand. "Ha! Fooled you!"

Jesse's surge of relief brought an urge to laugh, but Carla's reaction was far different. Her fear instantly morphed into anger. "That's not funny!" Her shout was loud enough to echo over the water. "I thought you were dead!"

"Take it easy, she didn't mean to scare you." He swam up beside Carla, putting a hand on her arm.

"No, I won't take it easy." She shook him off and glared at Cass. "She did intend to scare me, or she wouldn't have pretended to be floating like a dead body." Her gaze bored into Cassie's. "Don't you ever do something like that again. And you're grounded for a full week, understand?"

Cassie's face fell. Alecia was looking just as guilty as if they'd hatched the plan between them, but Carla kept her attention on their daughter.

"Stop yelling at me. I don't wanna live with you anymore. I'm going to live with Dad!" Cassie quickly swam away from them toward the boat.

Jesse winced at the child's response. Even he knew her desire to live with him was nothing more than a way to lash back at her mother. Carla's face was pale and set in stone as she swam back toward the boat as well with Alecia lagging behind.

He wasn't sure which way to go with this situation. Okay, yes, Cassie shouldn't goof around like that, yet on the other hand, he and his brothers had done much worse. Although most of the time they'd managed not to get caught, like when he'd sneaked out at night to visit Carla, which almost made him smile again.

The worst part of all was the way Cassie hadn't hesitated to play one parent off the other. Something he and his siblings had never done because his parents weren't separated or divorced and had always maintained a united front.

Which is what he should have done. He inwardly winced. Big mistake. No matter how he'd thought Carla had overreacted, he should have followed her lead in scolding Cassie for her prank.

"Let's eat lunch," Jesse said, trying to break the strained silence.

"I'm not hungry." Cassie pouted beside Alecia on one side of the boat, both girls wrapped in large brightly colored beach towels.

"That's fine, but I'm sure Alecia is." Jesse gestured to the food Carla had unpacked. "Help yourself, Alecia. There are brownies for dessert."

"Brownies!" Alecia's eyes lit up, and she eagerly went over to where Carla was making sandwiches. "Yum."

Cassie's sulk lasted for a good five minutes before she caved. "Can I have a sandwich?"

Jesse didn't answer, deciding this was between Carla and Cass.

"First, you need to apologize," Carla said. "I thought you might be dead, Cassie. Do you have any idea what that feels like? What you did was not one bit funny."

"I'm sorry." Cassie's expression was contrite. "I didn't mean to scare you or make you jump into the water with your clothes on."

"But you did. Not just me, but your dad, too." Carla let out a heavy sigh and gestured toward the food. "Apology accepted. Do you want ham or turkey?"

"Ham, please." Cassie leaned forward to snatch a grape from the fruit bowl.

"I'll have turkey," Alecia piped up. "Thanks, Ms. Templeton."

"You're welcome." To her credit, Carla didn't hold a grudge but made the girls sandwiches, added fruit to their paper plates, and provided them each a soft drink. The girls dug into the meal as if they hadn't eaten in weeks, making him smile.

Carla shivered a bit despite the warmth from the sun. He draped a towel over her shoulders. She nodded in thanks but didn't meet his gaze. Maybe he was wrong about her not holding a grudge.

She appeared to still be upset with him.

Because he hadn't instantly supported her. He wanted to explain that he was new at being a father but figured that could wait until they were alone.

"You want roast beef?" she asked him.

"That's great, thanks."

She made two more sandwiches, handing him one that was extra thick.

"When we're finished eating, we should head back," Carla said as she began closing up the food containers.

He hesitated. It was early, they'd only been out for ninety minutes, yet he understood she probably didn't want to sit around in wet clothes. He didn't mind stripping down to just wearing his swim trunks but sensed that wasn't going to fly with Carla.

"Why don't we go back for dry clothes, then spend more time on the lake?" he suggested. "I have the boat all afternoon."

"I don't think so." Carla's tone was firm. "Cassie has some chores to do around the house."

"Chores?" Their daughter let out a squeak of outrage. "Since when?"

"Since now." Her tone brooked no room for argument.

Cassie opened her mouth to argue, but Jesse shook his head at her with silent warning. This was not the time. Especially not in front of their guest.

He swallowed his own disappointment and nodded. "Whatever you say."

Carla shot him a quick, surprised glance, then continued with her task of cleaning up.

The picnic was quiet and subdued, the only lightness coming when the girls oohed and ahhed over Daisy's rich chocolate brownies.

When they were finished, he pulled up the anchor and started the boat. Once they were back in the McNally Bay Marina, Carla didn't hesitate to disembark, making sure Cassie and Alecia came with her.

He followed more slowly, not willing to let the day end

on a sour note. Carla and Cassie walked Alecia home, before turning toward her mother's house.

Once Cassie disappeared inside, with strict instructions to clean her room, Carla finally turned to face him.

"I'm sorry," he said quickly. "I should have supported you from the very beginning."

"Yes, you should have." She clutched the edges of the towel together as if she were still chilled. "You can't allow Cassie to play us off each other, like good cop, bad cop."

"I know, I get that." He spread his hands wide. "I'm learning, okay? I don't want to come between the two of you."

Carla stared at him for a long moment. "I think it's too late. She already knows hurting me is easy enough, all she has to do is threaten to live with you."

Their daughter's thoughtless words had struck deeper than he'd realized. "She didn't mean it."

Carla let out a harsh laugh. "Oh yes, she did. You've proven to be the fun one, while I'm the one forcing her to toe the line." Without saying anything else, Carla turned and went inside the house.

Leaving Jesse with the sick knowledge that he'd just lost a good portion of the ground he'd gained in the past five days with the two most important women in his life.

CARLA CHANGED HER CLOTHES, then did a small load of laundry with the towels and her wet things. Cass stomped around in her room, making a ton of noise while allegedly cleaning as she'd been told.

It was disheartening to know this was Carla's new reality. The beginning of Cassie playing one parent off the other.

The back-and-forth of a co-custody arrangement and an ongoing comparison of parenting style.

As a single mother, there were plenty of times she'd wished for a second adult to help, someone to bounce ideas off of and to talk things through with. It wasn't easy to handle everything alone. But in the end, every decision she'd made, right or wrong, had been hers alone. Surprisingly, her mother had gone along with that approach, playing the role of grandparent rather than trying to step in as someone in charge.

Now she had to find a way to add Jesse to the mix. Sure, he could claim to be new at parenting, but he should have followed her lead rather than once again try to undermine her authority.

It almost made her wish Jesse would move back to Chicago, keeping his visits here in McNally Bay to a minimum. It might be less disruptive all the way around.

She thought about talking to him later on, trying to set some things straight.

"Cass?" She poked her head into her daughter's room. It looked neat and clean, although Cassie's sullen expression hadn't changed. "I need you to fold the clothes and towels when the dryer is finished. After that, the dishwasher needs to be emptied, all the clean dishes put away. I'm heading back to the store."

"Fine." Cassie lifted her chin defiantly. "Just call me Cinderella."

"Okay, Cindy. Be back later." She turned and left the house without a moment of hesitation.

Cinderella. For the first time since she'd thought her daughter had drowned, a smile tugged at the corner of her mouth. The few chores Cassie had been told to do were nothing compared to what some kids her age were responsible for.

Although she knew plenty of others who weren't held accountable for anything.

Middle of the road, she decided. That was where she wanted Cassie to be. Not in grades, but in having responsibility. Like walking Bucky and doing chores while being grounded.

Carla came to an abrupt halt when she saw Dean Thomas standing on the corner of Main Street and Elmhurst, the street Templeton Grocery Store was located. The second he saw her, he took a step back, putting his hands up as if declaring his innocence.

"I'm not waiting for you, I promise." His face looked haggard as if he were still feeling the impact of his inebriated state from the night before. Honestly, she was surprised he'd been released from jail so soon. "I'm standing here, minding my own business."

She wasn't sure she believed him, although really it wasn't as if McNally Bay was a large city. Hers was the only grocery store in the area, so it was highly likely they'd continue to stumble across each other on a regular basis. She lifted her right wrist and ran the tips of her fingers over the bruises he'd left behind. "Good to hear. I'm sure you'll understand if I prefer not to have any more interactions with you."

His gaze tracked her gesture, and when he realized what he'd done, his face reddened with guilt. "I'm sorry."

She lifted a brow. "You should be."

"I was drunk." His tone sounded pitiful and a bit surly, and she knew then he wasn't nearly the man she'd thought he was.

"That's no excuse."

"I know." Without saying anything more, Dean quickly turned and headed off in the opposite direction from the grocery store. She watched him, hoping that he wasn't planning to return to the Bombay Pub and Grill for a repeat performance.

Maybe being arrested had scared him straight. She hoped so. She wanted this to be the end of his weirdly obsessive behavior toward her.

All this from one measly cup of coffee. No wonder she hadn't dated in the years since she'd given birth to Cassie.

Although, deep down, she knew the real reason was that none of the men around town lived up to what she had with Jesse.

The store was unusually busy, but with Sheryl's help, things went far more smoothly than usual. Once again, Carla felt she'd made the right decision to promote Sheryl to the assistant manager role.

Her mother was right, the third time was the charm.

When they'd finished going through the produce, weeding out the stuff that looked pathetic enough to never sell, Sheryl turned toward her. "Should we start working on the schedule now?"

"Not yet, let's finish up the inventory and purchase orders first. I can always spend time drafting a schedule later."

If Sheryl was disappointed, she didn't let on. They worked until dinnertime, then Carla told Sheryl to head home.

"We'll take turns staying late, so why don't you enjoy the evening with your boys? I'll stay late tonight, wrapping things up."

"Are you sure?" Sheryl looked torn. "I can stay tonight if that's better for you."

"You can stay tomorrow." When she realized that the following day was Saturday, she quickly added, "Don't worry, next weekend, we'll switch it up so you don't have every Saturday. I want this arrangement to work out for both of us."

"Me, too. Okay, thanks, Carla."

When she was alone in the office, she called home, but Cassie didn't answer the phone. Because she was still mad? Or because she'd disobeyed and left the house despite being grounded.

Muttering under her breath, she tried her mother's cell phone. Thankfully, she picked up. "Hi, Carla."

"Mom, are you with Cassie?"

"Yes, we're at Daisy's for dinner. Why?"

"I suppose Cassie didn't mention she was grounded."

"No, but she did mention all the chores were done that you'd asked her to do, so I thought that was the end of it. Besides, I hardly think having dinner at the diner with her grandmother is the same as hanging out with friends."

So now her mother decides to interfere with how she raised her daughter? Great, just great. "Fine, but afterward she needs to stay home, okay? I'm going to work late tonight but call if you need something."

"We'll be fine," her mother assured her.

"Where were you today?" Normally she didn't pry into her mother's personal life, but she was curious if she was still chatting with Leon Tate.

"Out with friends." Her mother's response sounded evasive. "Nothing for you to worry about."

"I'm not worried." What Carla really wanted to know was more about what Leon Tate had thought of Justin McNally's letter to Lucy, but it was clear her mother wasn't interested in sharing the details. At least, not in front of Cassie. "See you later."

"Of course."

Carla disconnected from the line and stared for a long moment at the stacks of invoices on her desk. Truthfully, she only had about an hour's worth of work to do before she needed to start on the schedule. But it wasn't long before she was called over to assist with a customer complaint. After that, she caught two teenagers shoplifting and had to wait for Deputy Garth Lewis to come arrest them. As closing time approached, she waited for all the employees to leave, then locked the door behind them, before returning to her office.

The invoices didn't take long, and when she finished, she went ahead and roughed out a schedule of shared responsibilities between her and Sheryl. She was satisfied at the thought of having more free time to spend with Cassie. Rising to her feet, she frowned, wrinkling her nose at the scent of smoke.

Was someone smoking cigarettes outside the grocery store? And if so, why was the scent so strong inside?

Carla crossed to her office door. She pushed on the handle, but the door didn't budge. There was no lock on the office door, she'd never needed one. And the door opened to the outside.

A shiver of fear trailed down her spine as she tried again with more force.

The door moved a fraction of an inch, but then stopped. There was something from the other side, something heavy preventing it from opening.

The scent of smoke grew stronger. She put a hand on the door, and the wood felt warm, confirming her suspicions that the fire was raging inside the grocery store, not outside it.

A fire that had been set on purpose, with something on the other side of the office preventing her escape.

She began to cough, wisps of smoke coming in from the gap beneath the door.

No! She quickly grabbed the phone off her desk and called 911, hoping and praying the deputies and volunteer firefighters would get here before it was too late.

14

Jesse walked up Main Street to the corner where the grocery store was located, trying to frame the conversation he needed to have with Carla. He didn't like knowing they were at odds, and honestly, he wanted to explain to her how much he cared about her.

How much he loved her.

Yet just blurting out the truth probably wasn't the way to go. Carla was skittish about their relationship, and the last thing he wanted to do was scare her off.

As he approached, he caught a glimpse of something yellow flickering through the window of the grocery store as he approached. He frowned, finding it odd that there may be a yellow lightbulb flashing on and off.

The wail of sirens had him glancing around curiously. Hearing sirens wasn't at all unusual in Chicago, but he thought this was the first time he'd heard them in McNally Bay. He knew from Garth that crime statistics around here were low.

Just another reason it was a good place to raise a child. To have a family.

A dark figure ducked out of the store door, wearing a hoodie up and over his head. Since it was well past eight, Jesse sprinted after him feeling certain the guy had been trying to steal something. "Hey! Stop!"

The figure glanced back at him at the same moment he reached the street lamp. The familiar facial features made him stumble. Brian? What was his partner doing here?

Jesse continued running, determined to find out. But as he moved past the store, he quickly realized the yellow light wasn't a bulb.

It was a fire inside the building.

Carla!

As much as he wanted to catch up to grab Brian, he couldn't leave if there was any chance Carla was trapped inside. With an abrupt move, he spun around and grabbed the door. It was locked.

He looked around, frantic for something that could be used to break in. The garbage bin! Without a second thought, he lifted the bulky garbage container and threw it as hard as he could through the glass window.

Glass shattered, and with the influx of air, the fire inside burned brighter. His heart thudded with fear, but he pulled up the collar of his T-shirt so that it covered his nose and mouth and pushed inside.

The sharp edge of glass cut his skin, but he ignored the pain, trying to see through the swirling smoke. He vaguely remembered Carla saying something about having an office, but where?

He had no clue.

The sirens were louder now, and he was relieved to know help was on the way. But the fire was growing bigger, spreading wider, and he feared if he didn't find Carla soon, it would be too late.

The fire was located in the paper products aisle, and as he scanned the area, he noticed there was a door almost directly behind the aisle, leading to a space in the back of the store.

Giving the fire a wide berth, he made his way through the back doorway, noticing there was a large rolling cart filled with canned goods parked in front of another door.

Eyes watering, he coughed as he leaned into the cart in an attempt to push it out of the way.

It didn't move.

What in the world? He could barely see but used his hands to feel around down by the wheels. When he realized there was a brake lever engaged, he released it and the one on the other side so he could push the cart away from the door.

"Carla?" He opened the door to what proved to be a tiny office area.

"Jesse?"

He'd never been so happy to hear his name. In the dim light, he could see her coming toward him. He reached out, snagged her arm, and pulled her close. "Yes, I'm here. Come on, let's get out of here."

She nodded, leaning against him. Her body convulsed with one racking cough after the next from the smoke surrounding them.

"This way," he said through the fabric of his shirt, steering her away from the source of the fire.

Several men wearing firefighting gear rushed toward them. "Is anyone else here?"

"No." Carla coughed again, then added, "Just me. I'm the one who called it in."

Jesse hadn't realized she'd been the one to call for assistance. The firefighters ushered them outside. Carla didn't seem to notice the shattered glass or pay attention to the destruction of her store. Whatever the fire hadn't damaged would be lost to water from the attempt to douse the flames.

The firemen took them out to the center of the parking lot, far away from the store, and made them sit down.

"Oxygen for both of you." The firefighter gave him a plastic face mask.

"Carla first," he croaked.

"She already has one." The firefighter's tone held a note of annoyance. "The ambulance should be here soon. You'll both need to be evaluated for smoke inhalation."

"Jesse? How did you know I was in trouble?" Carla asked, her voice hoarse and muffled from the oxygen mask.

"I didn't." But he quickly looked around for the sheriff's deputy. "I was coming to see you, Carla, when I noticed someone coming out of the store."

Her eyes widened, and she grasped his arm. "Dean Thomas?"

"No, actually it was my partner, Brian Malone." A fact he still hadn't quite come to grips with. "I'm sure he was the one who did this. He was wearing a dark sweatshirt with the hood pulled up over his head."

"That doesn't make sense. I don't understand."

Jesse didn't much understand it either, but now that Carla was safe, he felt as if he needed to focus on finding Brian. To hold his old friend and college roommate responsible for what he'd done.

Carla could have died. And for what? Just because Jesse wanted to move to McNally Bay? It didn't make sense. It wasn't as if the two of them were in the same city very often.

Garth Lewis rushed over, his gaze full of concern. "Carla, Jesse, I'm so glad you're both all right."

Carla wasn't even close to being all right judging by the sound of her cough. Where was the stupid ambulance? He grasped the deputy's arm. "Garth, listen. I witnessed Brian Malone, my business partner, coming out of the grocery store. I believe he set the fire. In fact, I'm starting to think he's been behind all of these attacks against me. Only this last time, he decided to go after the woman I love instead of directly coming at me."

"Okay, I'll send out a BOLO." Garth didn't try to second guess him. "Give me a description."

"Here's a picture." He used his phone to provide Garth Brian's likeness. Then Jesse filled him in, feeling a bit helpless because Brian didn't have much in the way of distinguishing marks or tattoos. In fact, it was no wonder Jesse hadn't noticed him before now, the guy had average features that would always blend into the crowd.

Thinking back, he was certain that Brian had been the one to smack him from the motorcycle. McNally Bay wasn't that far from Chicago. Brian had likely made the trip there and back in a day.

Wait a minute. He abruptly straightened. Who said Brian was in Chicago at all? The calls between them had been through their respective cell phones.

Was it possible Brian was staying in a hotel close by and had been from the very beginning? Coming in and out of McNally Bay at will? Had Brian even gone as far as infecting their own computer software system?

Why?

Garth was speaking into the radio on his collar, giving the name and description of the suspect related to the Templeton Grocery Store fire.

"Check the hotels in the area," he told Garth when he finished. "I think Brian has been here in or just outside of

McNally Bay the entire time. He must be the one who threw the brick at my car, and all the rest."

"Will do." Garth glanced once more at Carla. She was coughing less now, but Jesse was still concerned about the potential damage to her lungs. "Carla, do you want me to call your mom? She might hear about the fire."

"Oh, yes, please let her know I'm okay. In fact, there's no need to tell her I was inside the store. Just let her know I'm with Jesse and I'm fine."

Garth hesitated, then nodded. He walked back toward his squad and slid in behind the wheel. Seconds later, he was out of the parking lot, leaving nothing but dust in his wake.

Jesse wished he could go with him, but he refused to leave Carla.

If he hadn't decided to go meet her . . . He shuddered, unable to imagine what might have happened. Oh sure, the firemen had responded quickly, but without the broken glass, Jesse didn't think they would have known anyone was inside. And if they did know, they may have taken too long to find her, especially as she was locked in the back office.

Anger simmered at what Brian had done. Risking Carla's life for no good reason.

The ambulance pulled up, and two EMTs climbed out. Jesse insisted on Carla being treated first.

"I'm fine," she insisted. "My coughing is already better, see?"

The fact that her words were followed by another series of coughs did not help her case. Yet Jesse had a feeling she'd refuse to go to the hospital.

"I'm not leaving." Carla coughed again. "Bronson Methodist is too far away. My daughter needs me. Can't I just follow up in the clinic?"

Jesse opened his mouth to argue but caught sight of Irene Templeton and Cassie hurrying toward them.

"Carla! Are you all right?" Her mother appeared shaken at seeing Carla with an oxygen mask.

"I'm fine. You shouldn't have come." Carla's gaze went to Cassie.

The little girl flung herself into Carla's arms. "I'm sorry, Mom. I love you."

"I know, sweetie. I love you, too."

"What happened?" Irene demanded.

"It's my fault." Jesse removed the oxygen mask and rose to his feet. "Apparently, my business partner decided to target me and the people I care about. I saw him leaving the store, and I'm certain he started the fire."

"Jesse saved me, Mom," Carla spoke up. "He came right into the fire to save me."

For a long moment Irene stared incredulously, then surprised him by throwing her arms around him in a warm embrace.

"Thank you," she whispered against his chest. "Thank you for saving my daughter."

He awkwardly patted her back. "There's no need to thank me, Mrs. Templeton. I love Carla. I'd do anything for her. And for Cassie."

"You do?" Cassie asked.

Carla gaped at him from behind her oxygen mask. "You do?"

"Yeah, I do." He met Carla's gaze head-on, ignoring the others for a moment. "It's the main reason I'm moving to McNally Bay. I love you. And if it's too soon for you, that's fine. I'll wait until you're ready."

Carla didn't have a response to that, and he ignored the

pang around his heart that she hadn't said she was ready to love him right now.

"Well, I'm happy to hear that." Irene let him go, subtly wiping her eyes.

"You're going to live here, forever?" Cassie asked.

"That's right." He reluctantly tore his gaze from Carla to meet his daughter's. "But I don't want you to think that means you can be mean to your mother the way you were earlier today. From now on, I'm on your mother's side. What she says, goes, so don't even bother to try to get around us like that again."

"I won't." Cassie threw herself into his arms. "I'm glad you're staying, Dad."

He bent down to kiss the top of Cassie's head. "Me, too."

Carla didn't say anything, and he couldn't tell if the brightness in her eyes were tears of joy or a side effect of being in a smoky room.

This hadn't gone as planned, but he couldn't deny that having Irene hug and thank him was a win.

Now, all he needed to do was find a way to convince Carla to open her heart to him.

The most difficult task of all.

CARLA COULDN'T BELIEVE Jesse had proclaimed his love for her and that her mother had hugged him.

What was going on? Did the two of them have smoke-fried brain cells?

She wanted to believe that Jesse meant what he said, but she thought for sure that he'd spoken in the heat of the moment. Being stuck in her office with a fire raging on the other side of the door had been frightening.

And trusting Jesse meant what he'd said, that he'd truly stick around for the long haul, was equally terrifying.

She refused to go to the hospital, although agreed to keep using the oxygen as the firefighters put out the blaze. Her store was in shambles. Of course, they had insurance, but being out of business in the middle of summer would be a terrible blow financially.

She told herself not to think about it.

"Mrs. Templeton, why don't you take Cassie back home?" Jesse suggested. "It's late, and there's nothing more to do here. As soon as Carla feels up to it, I'll bring her home."

"Okay." Irene gave Carla a hug, then stepped back so Cassie could do the same.

Shortly after they left, a brown squad pulled up. Garth slid out from behind the wheel with a satisfied smile on his face. He jerked a thumb toward the vehicle. "Got your guy here, Jesse. You want to verify he's the one you saw?"

"Absolutely." Jesse approached the car and peered inside. "Yeah, that's Brian Malone. He's the one I saw running from the grocery store with the hood of his sweatshirt up over his head."

Carla's curiosity got the better of her. She took the oxygen mask off and joined Jesse. The guy in the back seat wore a sullen expression on his face and couldn't meet Jesse's eyes.

"Why, Brian? All this just because I planned to move to McNally Bay?"

Brian didn't answer.

"We've got him cold, Jesse. His clothes reek like turpentine, and I found the motorcycle he rented to get around town. With your testimony, he'll do time for arson and attempted murder."

Jesse curled his fingers into fists. Carla put a warning hand on his arm. "Don't, Jesse. He's not worth it."

"Why?" he asked again as if desperate to understand.

"I wanted you out working, not staying here for an entire week. I thought damaging your car would send you straight back to Chicago, but instead you decided to play house with the girl you knocked up years ago." Brian scowled and shrugged. "Don't you understand? We don't make money unless you're working."

"Me? What about you?"

Brian shook his head, then turned away. "I can't do the job like you," he finally admitted. "I tried and failed."

Carla suddenly understood. Their partnership wasn't really a partnership at all. Brian had been living off Jesse's skill all this time. "You leech," she said with disdain. "What did you do while Jesse was working hours and hours? Golf? Party? What?"

Brian shrugged. "I pretended to have jobs so he wouldn't figure out that I wasn't doing anything other than maintaining our finances."

Jesse appeared stunned speechless at the news. After a long moment, he spoke. "You infected our computer software, didn't you?"

Brian tipped his chin to his chest, which was answer enough.

Garth stepped closer. "That's enough. Jesse, you'll be able to bring a fraud case against him if you'd like, but for now, I'm taking him in for these recent crimes."

"Go ahead." Jesse took a step back. "I'm done talking to him."

Garth slid in behind the wheel and drove off, taking Brian Malone to the Clark County jail.

"I can't believe it," Jesse murmured. "My friend, my

partner did this. Just to hide the fact that he was incompetent and living off me."

"Oh, Jesse." She put her arm around his waist and gave him a quick hug. "I'm sorry that it turned out this way. I was sure that Dean Thomas was the one behind this. I even saw him earlier today."

Jesse drew her close, and she realized that both of their clothing still reeked of smoke. "I hate knowing that you were put in danger because of me."

"I'm fine, and so are you." Her heart ached for the sense of betrayal he must be feeling. "We'll get through this, Jesse, together."

"Together," he repeated. He tugged her closer so that she was fully in his arms. "I need you, Carla. More than you can possibly know. Being here with you like this makes me feel like I've come home. Not because of McNally Bay, but because of you. And Cassie. But mostly, you."

"Oh, Jesse. I need you, too." And suddenly she realized how much she loved him. Had never really stopped loving him. And it seemed cruel not to tell him. "And I love you."

He froze, his muscles going tense. "What did you say?"

"I love you." She pulled out of his embrace enough to look him in the eye, the swirling red and white lights from the fire trucks illuminating his wary features. "If you want to know the truth, I've always loved you. I tried dating over the years, but each time was a colossal failure."

"I don't want to rush you," he protested, but she shushed him.

"Just listen, okay? No man ever measured up to you, Jesse. Your family seemed so wonderful compared to mine. Mostly because me and my dad, well, we didn't have a close relationship."

"I remember you saying that nine years ago," he admitted.

"Yes, and the night I told him I was pregnant," she paused, coughed, then pushed on, "he slapped me across the face and told me the father had better not be one of those no-good McNallys. Less than five minutes later, he clutched his chest and went down like a rock."

"Oh, Carla." Jesse pulled her close. "That must have been terrible."

"I couldn't save him," she admitted. "Telling him I was pregnant caused him to suffer a deadly heart attack. The guilt over what we had done was overwhelming. I knew then that he died being angry and disgusted with me, worse than usual. And there was nothing I could do to change it. For years I wanted my dad's attention. For him to care about me. To be proud of me. But instead, I pretty much killed him."

For a long moment, Jesse simply held her. "I'm sorry," he whispered. "So sorry that you had to go through that alone."

She shrugged. "Looking back, I don't think it was all my fault, but it sure felt that way at the time. For years I told myself Cassie was better off without you. Without a father. But deep down, I knew that wasn't true. When you returned to McNally Bay, my heart filled with hope and dread. Hope because you looked better than ever, and dread because I thought for sure you'd leave me again. I guess that's why I was so determined not to risk my heart by giving you a second chance."

"Carla." His voice was low and husky. He bent and kissed her long and hard. "I'm sorry I hurt you back then, but please know that I love you very much."

"I know, and I love you, too." She hesitated, then added, "And I love the way you're already forging a great relationship with Cassie. Very different than the one I had with my father. I want her to know what it's like to have a father who loves and cares about her. Who supports her even when things go wrong."

"Carla, you're so wonderful, so special. I'm so honored you're willing to give us a chance."

"I'm not special."

"That's your father talking, not me. You are very special." He kissed her again, and she clung to him, never wanting to let go.

Carla knew her heart belonged to Jesse McNally, now and forever. The grocery store was a mess, and his software company was, too.

Yet none of that mattered as long as they had each other.

EPILOGUE

T*hree weeks later...*

It took Jesse longer than he'd anticipated to go through all the business financial statements, proving that Brian had been living off the money Jesse alone had earned. Brian had lied about how much they were being paid by each client and spent the difference on himself, putting the money under names of fake clients. Jesse couldn't believe there was almost fifty thousand in Brian's personal account, all money Jesse had earned, but as much as it galled him, he decided to let it go. No doubt a bulk of the cash would end up going to his former partner's criminal defense lawyer.

Jesse dissolved Software Solutions, Inc. and created a new company named Software Rescue, LLC. Jesse figured he could run the company out of his home, a new and different house he'd found located on the opposite side of town from the McNallys' B&B. He'd continued searching for a place after the Kaplans made it clear they weren't going to sell. Besides, he'd wanted something bigger and closer to the lake.

Obviously, he was more high maintenance than he'd thought.

After reviewing the finances, he knew he could cut his travel in half, providing more support to Carla and Cassie since Brian wouldn't be living off him any longer.

It was hard to accept that his old friendship was gone. Or, really, had never been. When he thought back to the five years he'd worked nonstop for the company, only to be taken advantage of, he saw red. But it the attack on Carla was so much worse than what Brian had done to him personally.

He found Carla at the new house that they were in the process of moving into. Seeing her helped improve his mood.

"Hey." He swept her up into his arms for a deep kiss. "I missed you."

"I missed you, too." She pulled back, searching his gaze. "Are you okay?"

"Just mad about being played for a fool." He glanced over her shoulder. "Where's Cass? I thought she was going to help you clean things up here."

"At Alecia's with Bucky. You need to know, Daisy pulled me aside and asked if it was okay for her to give Bucky to Cassie as a gift. She said that she underestimated how much time and attention a puppy needed, and it was too much for her to do while running the diner."

"Really? I'm sure Cassie is thrilled."

Carla shook her head with a rueful smile. "Jesse, I didn't tell Cassie yet because that's a decision we need to make together, before giving our permission."

"Oh." He was humbled she'd included him and remembered they'd promised to maintain a united front. "I'm all for it, if you are."

"I am. And you're right, Cassie will be ecstatic." She tilted her head, her expression turning thoughtful. "Jesse, don't hold on to your anger at Brian. He's not worth it."

"Not easy," he countered, his brow furrowed. There were times he still couldn't believe the man he'd lived with for their entire four years of college had turned on him.

"I know, but think about how much my mom hated your family, the way my dad did, too. Do you think it's worth holding on to a grudge for that long?"

He blew out his breath, hating to admit she had a point. "Okay, you're right. I'm thrilled that your mother doesn't hate me anymore." Since Cassie wasn't around, he took Carla's hand and pulled her out onto the fancy deck that overlooked Lake Michigan. The house was big enough to add several kids, but still not even close to the price of his downtown Chicago condo, which had sold in record time for more than he'd expected. "Come outside for a minute."

"All right." She followed him onto the deck, gazing at the rippling blue water. "I still can't believe you spent so much money on this place."

"You're worth it." He cleared his throat, pulled the ring box out of his pocket, and then dropped to one knee. He held up the ring. "Carla Templeton, I love you with all my heart and soul. You've always been the only woman for me, except that I was too stupid to realize it. Will you please marry me? Soon? So we can live together with Cassie and Bucky as a family?"

He'd tried not to go too overboard with the ring, knowing that something modest yet elegant would be closer to Carla's taste. It didn't matter as she barely glanced at it, her gaze locked on his. "Yes, Jesse. I will marry you as soon as you'd like. But I have to warn you, your sister's gazebo is booked solid with weddings from now through September."

"Then maybe we can get married here, on the deck, overlooking the water." He hoped his tone didn't sound too much like he was begging, even though he was. "I don't want to wait, Carla. We can have a small ceremony here, without all the fuss. I want Cassie to have a full-time father."

When she didn't respond right away, he realized that women liked to fuss, especially about something as important as a wedding. "Never mind, that was a stupid idea. Of course, you'll want everything to be just right. We'll wait until October."

"No, Jesse, I like your idea of getting married right here." She swept her hand out as if encompassing everything. "A new life in our new home."

His heart soared. "You pick the date and the time, and I'll be there." He rose to his feet and swept her in for another hug, lifting her clear off her feet. "I love you, Carla. Thanks for everything you've done for Cassie over the years."

"No more looking back," she admonished. "From this point forward, we're going enjoy today while focusing on our future."

"Deal." He set her back on her feet, then cuddled her close as they gazed out over the water.

He couldn't ask for anything more than what he had right here.

Dear Reader,

I hope you enjoyed the fourth book in my McNally Series. Thank you to all of you who have sent me messages about how much you're enjoying the McNallys. Jesse's story is one of forgiveness and looking forward, two traits that as a nurse I feel are very important in life.

As always, reviews are critical for authors, so if you enjoyed this story, please take a moment to leave a review. I would be very grateful! Also, I love hearing from my readers. I can be contacted via my website www. laurascottbooks.com, through Facebook at Laura Scott Author, and on Twitter @laurascottbooks.

Also, if you enjoy my books, take a moment to sign up for my newsletter via my website. I offer an exclusive novella that isn't for sale anywhere, only to each of my newsletter subscribers.

Lastly, I'm hard at work on Jeremy's story. If you're curious about the second eldest member of the McNally family, keep reading for a sneak peek at the first chapter of *To Believe*.

Sincerely,

Laura Scott

TO BELIEVE

Jeremy McNally scowled at the driver in the car in front of him. The guy—or woman, it was hard to tell—had crossed the center line twice in the past five miles.

Two times too many.

Highway ZZ was the main highway that snaked through Clark County, leading from his home, Lansing, Michigan, and going all the way to McNally Bay. It also had a lot of curves and hills, making it dangerous under the best circumstances. Driving as the sun went down, with no street lights anywhere in the vicinity wasn't optimal. Jeremy tried to stay far enough back to avoid getting close to the erratic driver, without losing sight of him.

When the driver crossed the center line for a third time, Jeremy cued up his phone using the hands-free functionality and requested a call to 911.

"I have reason to believe the driver of the Ford pickup truck, license plate SRY-555 heading west on highway ZZ is driving under the influence. He's crossed the center line three times, and I'm concerned he's going to hit someone."

"I'll send a deputy to your location," the dispatcher

replied. "Please don't try to engage the suspect on your own."

"Yeah, well, you'd better hurry." Jeremy disconnected from the call, knowing that if the Clark County Sheriff's Deputy didn't get there soon, he would absolutely engage the suspect on his own.

Anything to avoid another horrific tragedy.

He glanced momentarily at his heavily scarred hands, the result of being hit by a drunk driver nine months ago.

The same crash had cost him his career as a trauma surgeon.

Jeremy did his best to push those thoughts aside. He kept his gaze on the battered Ford, tightening his grip on the steering wheel when he watched the idiot cross the center line once again.

If that yahoo driver turned off the highway, he was going to follow him. No way was he going to let this son-of-a-gun get away unscathed. Whoever was driving had no right to be behind the wheel in whatever condition they were in.

It was another five miles before he saw the reassuring red and blue flashing lights approaching from behind. As the wailing siren grew louder, he dropped back, putting more distance between his vehicle and the one in front of him so the deputy could get close to the Ford.

The police car passed him, providing a glimpse of a red haired female deputy behind the wheel.

He had nothing against female cops and knew she was probably well trained, but it worried him a bit that she'd be facing the driver on her own. Small towns like McNally Bay didn't have a large police presence, which meant cops drove alone, without a partner.

Not his problem, he reminded himself. Didn't he have enough issues of his own to worry about? First the drunk driving crash, then multiple surgeries on his hands, the loss of his career, then Phoebe Sanders leaving him for one of his colleagues, another surgeon.

One that could still operate, making the big bucks she so clearly desired.

Whatever. He pushed the thoughts away to watch the scene unfold in front of him. It took several minutes for the Ford pickup to slow down and pull over to the side of the road, with the deputy pulling in directly behind him. Jeremy found himself slowing down and parking along the side of the highway, too. He was a witness to the erratic driving. The cop might find it helpful to take his statement.

He didn't move from his vehicle, though. The red haired deputy got out from her squad and cautiously approached the Ford's driver's side door. The sun was low on the horizon, and with the trees lining the road, it seemed darker than normal. She put the beam of her flashlight directly on the suspect.

The additional light enabled Jeremy to see the deputy more clearly, and this time, he recognized her. Trina Waldorf, younger sister of Steve Waldorf, the guy he'd hung out with for a couple of weeks one summer in McNally Bay many years ago.

Steve had been twenty, Jeremy twenty-one at the time. He remembered they hadn't appreciated Steve's seventeen-year-old sister tagging along wherever they went. Trina had been cute, and Jeremy might have been interested in getting to know her better, if not for the fact that Steve had made it perfectly clear that Trina was off-limits.

Not my sister, man. Keep your grimy hands to yourself. Capisce?

Steve was always using Italian phrases like that. His mother had been Italian, and he'd claimed she taught him everything she knew. Jeremy noticed that Trina hadn't tossed Italian phrases around and figured Steve was just trying to show off.

He'd kept his distance from the cute Trina. He and Steve had shared some good times that summer, before they'd both gone their separate ways. And it made him wince to realize he hadn't thought about Steve in the ten years since.

Until now. And only because of Trina.

He rolled down his window to listen as Trina spoke to the driver. "Sir, I need you to step out of the vehicle."

Trina gestured to the driver and the guy, more like a young kid about twenty, pushed the door open and stumbled out. The driver was skinny with long greasy hair.

"Turn around and place your hands on the truck," she continued, still holding the flashlight with one hand, her other resting on her thick utility belt.

Skinny moved as if to turn around, but then abruptly lashed out at Trina, hitting her with his fist. The blow connected with her shoulder. She stumbled back a step. Jeremy instantly pushed out of his car, why, he wasn't sure, other than instinctively feeling as if she needed back up.

Even if a former surgeon with busted hands wouldn't be much help.

But Trina didn't back off after being assaulted. Instead, she pulled something out of her belt and aimed it at Skinny. Two barbs on coils shot out and embedded themselves in Skinny's chest through the thin ratty fabric of his T-shirt. Jeremy had to smile with satisfaction when he realized she'd tased him. With the amount of juice those things packed, he felt certain Skinny would go down like a rock.

Only he didn't. Skinny let out a howl and rushed directly toward Trina, arms outstretched so that he looked like a Frankenstein out of a horror flick.

"Look out!" Jeremy shouted.

Trina was one step ahead of Skinny. She pulled her baton with a practiced move and cracked it along his shoulder and head.

This time, Skinny did drop to his knees, swaying there for a minute before collapsing face forward onto the asphalt. Trina didn't waste a second, she pulled her cuffs off her belt and yanked one arm, then the other to latch the cuffs around his wrists.

"Timothy Eden, you're under arrest for driving under the influence, assaulting a police officer, and resisting arrest." Trina took a deep breath, then glanced over at him as if noticing his presence for the first time. "Sir, I'm going to need you to return to your vehicle."

"Trina, it's me, Jeremy McNally. You know, Steve's friend?" He felt foolish introducing himself since it was clear she didn't remember him. And yeah, that stung. "I'm the one who called this in."

"I see." She nodded at him, her gaze difficult to read. "I appreciate that, thanks. But really, Jeremy, you should move on. I've got this."

"I know you do, and I'm impressed." He didn't step back but glanced at Skinny who was moaning pitifully from his prone position on the asphalt. "I don't understand why the Taser didn't take him down. I've seen them in action in the emergency department, usually they're very effective."

"Yeah, well, not so much when your perp is hyped up on crystal meth. Somehow that stuff gives weaklings like this guy a superhuman strength." She rubbed her shoulder for a moment as if reliving the moment she'd been sucker punched, then reached down and grasped Skinny, aka Timothy Eden, by his cuffed wrists. "Come on, get up. On your feet. Now!"

Jeremy moved out of the way as Trina half carried, half pushed Skinny toward her vehicle. Without another word to Jeremy, she secured Skinny in the back caged area of the squad, then slid in behind the wheel.

She was gone before he could say anything more.

Trina hoped Jeremy hadn't noticed how badly her hands were shaking. Not from the impact of Eden's fist against her shoulder, although the blow had hurt, but because of seeing Jeremy again.

The minute he'd spoken, she'd recognized his deep husky voice. Why wouldn't she? She'd had a big crush on Jeremy McNally that summer ten years ago. One-sided puppy love on her part, mere tolerance on his.

For a moment, the image of her older brother, her idol, flashed in her memory. The way Steve had looked that summer, young and healthy, so full of life. His grin full of mischief and glee. He'd always been so protective of her. Steve had been sweet, kind, and caring.

Before he'd gotten hooked on drugs.

Before he'd died.

She wondered if Jeremy knew that Steve had passed away six years ago. The way he'd introduced himself as Steve's friend made her think he had no clue.

But he should have. If he'd cared at all about her brother, he absolutely should have known Steve was dead.

Whatever. She shook her head in an effort to dislodge the image. After Steve's downward spiral into the abyss of drug addiction, she'd made it her mission to help eradicate drug manufacturing from the rural area of Clark County. It was her way of honoring her brother's memory.

Yet she was forced to reluctantly admit that it was thanks to Jeremy's 911 call that she'd been able to grab Eden tonight. Having a meth-head in custody was a good start. The minute the drugs in Eden's system wore off she was sure he'd be more than willing to start talking about where the current meth lab was located.

If he knew the location at all. Which she hoped, prayed he did.

She'd gotten close before, but the brains behind the crystal meth lab used a trailer that made the entire operation portable, so they could move from one location to the next in less than an hour. Even worse, there were plenty of places to hide. Clark County was spread across hundreds of wooded acres, and there were only eight full-time deputies, including herself, and one part-timer to patrol the area.

It made looking for the current meth lab akin to finding a smelt in the depths of Lake Michigan.

With Eden in custody, she felt certain they'd find the elusive trailer. Bringing in the brains behind the entire drug operation would be an added bonus. Someone who, she felt certain, wasn't hooked on drugs but didn't hesitate to profit off those who were.

Like Steve.

As she headed toward headquarters where their small Clark County jail was housed, her thoughts turned back to Jeremy. Why was he back in McNally Bay? She'd caught a glimpse of him from afar seven weeks ago when he'd returned for Jazz and Dalton's wedding, but he hadn't noticed her.

Mostly because she'd made it a point to stay far away.

Then it hit her. Of course. Jeremy must be back for Jemma and Garth's wedding. Garth Lewis was another Clark County Deputy, and she knew he was getting married on

Saturday in the gazebo overlooking Lake Michigan to Jemma McNally, Jeremy's younger sister.

A small cozy family-oriented ceremony that Garth had invited her to attend as a guest.

She swallowed a groan. Wasn't that just peachy? There would be no way to avoid the obligation to chat and socialize with Jeremy before the wedding and again at the reception.

Unless she decided not to attend.

Garth would be hurt by her backing out at the last minute. They'd grown close working together over the past few years, and he'd often treated her like the younger sister he'd never had. And in some ways, he'd been the older brother she'd lost.

It was tempting, oh so tempting to avoid contact with Jeremy McNally. Frankly, she'd been surprised when he'd recognized her, but the fact was, she and Jeremy barely knew each other. They had shared a brief interaction two weeks out of one summer ten years ago. No big deal.

Except to her. In more ways than one.

She blew out her breath in a heavy sigh. Time to pull on her big girl panties and get over it. What did it matter after all this time anyway? Jeremy was some hot-shot surgeon now, a man way out of her league.

Besides, her crush had ended when she'd realized he was partially responsible for the beginning of Steve's spiral into alcohol and drugs. Ten years ago, the night before their parents were heading home to Detroit, she'd sneaked out and caught Steve and Jeremy drinking beer around the beach campfire. Jeremy was twenty-one, so she knew he must have been the one who'd bought the six-pack. And of course, her brother hadn't possessed the strength of will to say no.

It wasn't until much later, when she'd found Steve strung out on drugs, that she'd really understood the significance of that night. She believed that Steve hadn't done any drinking until he'd hung out with Jeremy. And the addiction hadn't ended there.

Old news. Besides, she had to admit that drinking a few beers was one thing, while using crystal meth was something entirely different. Yet illogical as it might be, she couldn't help wondering if Jeremy hadn't bought the six-pack that night and hadn't encouraged Steve to spend his last night in McNally Bay drinking by the fire, that her brother may not have wandered down the wrong path.

Might have avoided the horrible spiral that eventually had taken his life. Four months after his twenty-fourth birthday, her brother had died of a drug overdose.

And her life had never been the same.

"Get me out of here." Eden's pathetic voice intruded on her emotional thoughts.

"Soon. Lucky for you, we're almost at the jail." She glanced at him through her rearview mirror. Eden was bleeding from his head wound, blood dripping down his face, matting in his greasy hair and staining his shirt. Ugh. Most cops understood the danger of tangling with a meth-head, she hadn't been lying to Jeremy about their super-human strength. But now, looking at her injured perp, she wondered if she might need Jeremy's statement to prove she'd acted in self-defense.

These days, more and more people were more worried about the perps who were injured while getting arrested than they were about law enforcement officers who put their lives on the line every day.

She pulled up in front of the main entrance to the building, then went around to pull Eden from the squad. The guy couldn't walk straight, and she hoped that was because of the drugs, not the blow to his head.

Getting Jeremy's statement was looking more necessary by the minute.

She was surprised to find Deputy Alex Rhine chatting with Emily Hart, the dispatcher. The moment Alex saw her, he straightened from his perch and hurried over to help.

"Hey, Trina, are you okay?"

She appreciated how Alex instantly went to her defense, knowing she wouldn't have used force against Eden unless she absolutely needed to.

"Yeah, he hit my shoulder, but that was after he was tased, so I had to use the baton to subdue him."

Alex whistled under his breath. "Must be high on something."

"Crystal meth, judging by the looks of his teeth. And when I pulled his license plate, this is not his first drug offense. He was busted just a few months ago for the same thing." She pushed Eden toward the jail cell. "We need to call someone in to take his blood for a drug test, then book him for driving under the influence as a second offense, assaulting an officer, and resisting arrest."

"You got it." Alex took Eden from her and wrestled the guy into the cell. He glanced over his shoulder. "I heard on the radio you were bringing someone in, so I thought I'd come in to help."

"I appreciate that." She was relieved to have Alex's help with Eden. Her shoulder was throbbing now, and she hoped the idiot hadn't injured her shoulder to the point she might need surgery.

"No problem. Although looking at you now, I wish I'd gone to the scene." Alex's gaze was full of concern as he looked at her. "Do you need to leave early? I can ask Emily to call someone working the graveyard shift in early."

"Who's on? Nathan Beck and Kevin Powell?" Both guys were decent enough cops, but Nathan in particular didn't think much of female cops and was very set in his ways. She highly doubted he'd come in early for her. And Kevin was going through a rough patch with his wife and had two small kids. "Nah, don't bother. It's only another couple of hours."

"Okay, then you stay here with this guy, and I'll hit the patrols." Alex headed toward the door, stopping abruptly when it swung open. "Hey, buddy, we're not open for walk-ins, you need to come back in the morning."

"I'm not here for myself, but to provide a witness statement."

She caught her breath when she saw Jeremy standing there, his hands tucked into the pockets of his well-worn jeans, the yellow polo shirt stretched across his muscular chest. He looked bigger in the bright lights of their head-quarters, more handsome than she remembered, with his brown hair cut short and piercing green eyes. "I witnessed an assault on a police officer and want to be sure my side of the story is on record."

Trina felt her jaw drop in shock. Was Jeremy a mind reader now? How did he know that she'd thought about asking him to provide support for what had happened on highway ZZ?

It was becoming evident that avoiding Jeremy while he was here in McNally Bay would be impossible.

www.ingramcontent.com/pod-product-compliance
Lightning Source LLC
Chambersburg PA
CBHW050409190726
48284CB00007BB/2490